DOCTOR WHO
FEAR DEATH BY WATER

FEAR DEATH BY WATER

EMILY COOK

BBC BOOKS

UK | USA | Canada | Ireland | Australia
India | New Zealand | South Africa

BBC Books is part of the Penguin Random House group of companies whose addresses can be found at global.penguinrandomhouse.com

Penguin Random House UK
One Embassy Gardens, 8 Viaduct Gardens, London SW11 7BW

penguin.co.uk
global.penguinrandomhouse.com

First published by BBC Books in 2025

Copyright © Emily Cook 2025
The moral right of the author has been asserted.

No part of this book may be used or reproduced in any manner for the purpose of training artificial intelligence technologies or systems. In accordance with Article 4(3) of the DSM Directive 2019/790, Penguin Random House expressly reserves this work from the text and data mining exception.

Doctor Who is produced in Wales by Bad Wolf with BBC Studios Productions.
Executive Producers: Jane Tranter, Julie Gardner, Joel Collins,
Phil Collinson and Russell T Davies

Editorial Director: Albert DePetrillo
Project Editor: Steve Cole
Cover Design: Lee Binding
Map Design: Abigail Scarfe
Typeset by Rocket Editorial Ltd

Printed and bound in Great Britain by Clays Ltd, Elcograf S.p.A.

The authorised representative in the EEA is Penguin Random House Ireland, Morrison Chambers, 32 Nassau Street, Dublin D02 YH68

A CIP catalogue record for this book is available from the British Library

ISBN 9781785949616

Penguin Random House is committed to a sustainable future for our business, our readers and our planet. This book is made from Forest Stewardship Council® certified paper.

Contents

Prologue		1
Chapter 1	The Lighthouse Keeper's Daughter	7
Chapter 2	The Oncoming Storm	13
Chapter 3	In the Cold Light of Night	21
Chapter 4	Rocky Horror Show	25
Chapter 5	The Ship's Graveyard	33
Chapter 6	John Smith and the Common Men	43
Chapter 7	The Mind's Eye	51
Chapter 8	The Dead Sea	63
Chapter 9	Feats of Female Fortitude	71
Chapter 10	The Subconscious Monster	79
Chapter 11	The Twilight Zone	87
Chapter 12	Force of Nature	97
Chapter 13	Blast to Kingdom Come	107
Chapter 14	Circle of Life	115
Chapter 15	Ultraviolet	123
Chapter 16	The Lady of the Rock	131
Chapter 17	When Life Gives You Potatoes	143
Chapter 18	Amazing Grace	151
Chapter 19	Sir Duke	155
Chapter 20	Time and Tide	163
Epilogue		169

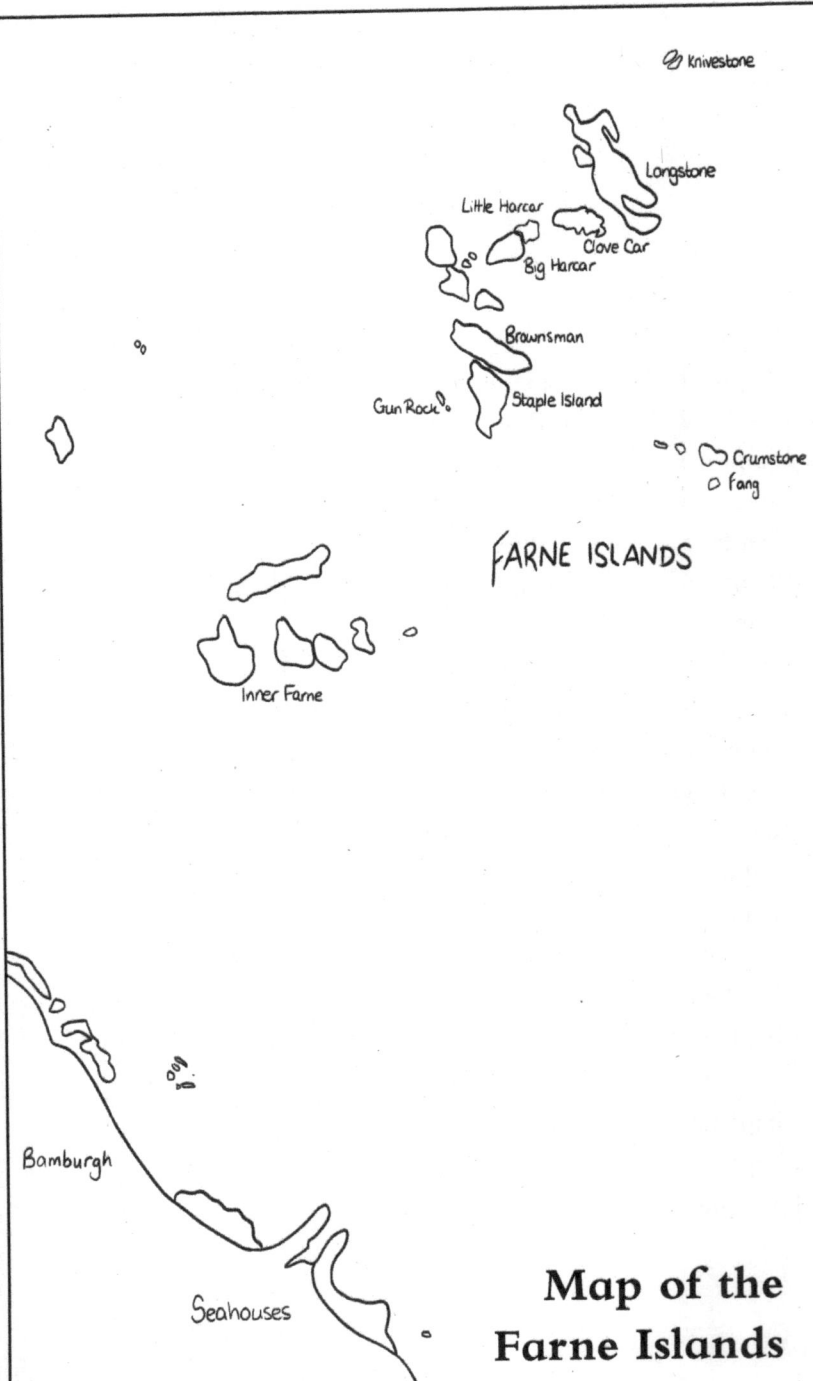

*For Mum and Dad, who are my rock,
my inspiration and my guiding light.*

*And for Grace Horsley Darling,
and all the souls she saved at sea.*

Prologue

4 July 2000
RNLI Grace Darling Museum, Bamburgh, Northumberland

'Excuse me? Do you work here?'

'Me?' said the tall man browsing the mugs in the gift shop. He had big brown eyes, a very impressive coat and the most dazzling smile. 'No. I'm just visiting. Do *you* work here?'

'I can't work here. I'm seven.'

'Nice to meet you, Seven. I'm the Doctor.'

'Nooo,' the girl giggled. 'My name is Emily.'

'Emily, what did we teach you about talking to strangers?' said a stern voice, coming alongside. Emily ignored her teacher and continued chatting.

'My name's not seven, I just *turned* seven.'

'Best age, seven!' the Doctor raved. 'You've peaked! Wait, no, scratch that, you've always got your best years ahead of you. Isn't that right, Miss?'

'Yes, I suppose so,' Miss Bowers replied reluctantly.

'You've got to keep living,' the Doctor continued. 'Keep rocking and rolling through life. Oh, you should try *cheese*-rolling, Seven. It's the best fun!'

Emily giggled again, enjoying this stranger's strangeness. 'I only *eat* cheese,' she said.

'Well, you are looking at the Cooper's Hill Cheese-Rolling Champion 2024. Thanks to a robust round of Double Gloucester.' The Doctor grinned. 'Spectacular cheese, Double Gloucester!'

'I like Edam best,' said Emily. 'What cheese do you like, Miss?'

'Stilton,' said Miss Bowers matter-of-factly.

'Yuck!' said the Doctor.

'It's delicious with pears.'

'Double yuck!'

'Come on now, Emily, enough of this,' said Miss Bowers, ushering her charge out of the gift shop and through the small circular exhibition room, past a tall model lighthouse. 'We need to catch up with the rest of the class.'

'What class are you in?' asked the Doctor, following them, much to Miss Bowers' disapproval.

'Year 3,' said Emily. 'We're learning about the Victorians.'

'The Victorians!' exclaimed the Doctor. 'You know, I met Queen Victoria once. And a werewolf. On the same day.'

'What?!' asked Emily.

'Just ignore him,' said Miss Bowers, as they joined the other pupils. They congregated around an old preserved poster which read:

A VISIT TO THE HEROINE GRACE HORSLEY DARLING AT LONGSTONE ISLAND.

'So,' said Miss Bowers, calling her class to attention, 'Year 3, what do you remember about Grace Darling?'

'She lived in a lighthouse,' said Emily, 'and one day she helped her father save nine people who were shipwrecked. She was very brave.'

'Yes, she was Victorian Britain's most celebrated heroine!' Miss Bowers agreed. 'And over here, we can see Grace Darling's boat.'

'Wow!' exclaimed Emily. 'Her *actual* boat?'

'It's a 21-foot Northumberland coble,' said Miss Bowers, reading the information board, 'which is a type of old wooden rowing boat. It inspired some of the earliest lifeboat designs. Amazing, right? Now look at this…' The students turned round to face the glass cabinet their teacher was pointing at. 'These are locks of Grace's hair. They're bleached blonde from exposure over the years, but Grace's hair was brown.'

'Why did they keep her hair like that?' Emily asked.

'We all want something to remember our heroes by, right? Back in the 1800s, one of the best ways of remembering someone was to ask for a piece of their hair. Grace sent her locks to people all over the country. Everyone wanted a piece of Grace Darling.'

Next to the glass cabinet was a display containing some of Grace's correspondence, tinged yellow with age.

'What's this?' asked one of the other children, skipping on to the next exhibit.

'This is Mr Darling's barometer, Josie,' said Miss Bowers.

'What's a barometer?'

'It's an instrument that measures atmospheric pressure,' Miss Bowers explained. 'The Darlings would have used it to help forecast the weather.'

'Why's it making that buzzing noise?' Emily wondered aloud.

'Hmmm, that's weird…' said the Doctor, who had joined them at the exhibit. He was holding a gadget of some sort. Emily wasn't sure what it was, but it looked a bit like a computer mouse. The Doctor was waving it around the barometer and talking to it.

All of a sudden, a pulse of energy emitted from the barometer, slightly shaking the adjacent exhibits.

'What *was* that?' Emily gasped.

'Good question!' said the Doctor.

'Is there an earthquake, Miss?' asked Josie.

'Settle down, children,' said Miss Bowers, looking around for a member of staff and an explanation. Meanwhile, Emily crouched down and carefully retrieved a piece of paper that had fallen from its exhibition frame. It was a letter, written in Grace's distinctive cursive script; it must have been tucked away behind the one on display, forgotten.

Or hidden.

Fear Death by Water

'Can I see that?' said the Doctor, gently taking the page from her hand. *'Since the rescue, I have suffered from an affliction beyond my comprehension,'* he read. *'The most terrifying vision – the blazing eyes of a beast in the ocean – is consuming my thoughts...'* He must have noticed the concern on Emily's face, because he suddenly put on a happier voice: 'Or at least it was until a funky unicorn appeared and made the beast happy again and I woke up from my bad dream and felt much better, The End.' With a wink at Emily and a pantomime wipe of his forehead, he slipped the letter into his pocket and turned back to the barometer. 'Artron energy,' he muttered, lost in his thoughts again. 'There's *definitely* Artron energy on this barometer. And it reacted to my sonic. Why?'

'What's Artron energy?' Emily asked.

Miss Bowers glared at the Doctor, then flashed Emily a look not to engage with this strange man interfering with the exhibits. 'He's just being silly. Artron energy doesn't exist.'

'That's the trouble with grown-ups,' said the Doctor, frowning as he read his gadget. 'They stop believing in things. And they start liking blue cheese.'

'You're a grown-up,' Emily pointed out.

'Oh, really?' The Doctor pulled a funny face.

Emily giggled. Miss Bowers rolled her eyes.

'I'm old and I'm wise,' said the Doctor stoically, 'but I am most definitely silly too. And I'm certainly never a grown-up.'

Emily looked up at him.

'You don't look *that* old...'

'Age is relative.' The Doctor crouched down and whispered into Emily's ear a number too large for her seven-year-old brain to fully comprehend.

Emily gasped. 'No. Way! He's older than you, Miss!'

'Don't sound *so* surprised,' said Miss Bowers, folding her arms.

'How are you not dead?' asked Emily, turning back to the Doctor.

But Emily never got her answer; the Doctor had gone.

Chapter One
The Lighthouse Keeper's Daughter

6 September 1838
The Farne Islands, Northumberland, England

On a small remote island in the North Sea, a few miles off the cliff of Bamburgh on the Northumberland coast, a young woman hummed merrily to herself as she loaded her wooden rowing boat with a sack of potatoes fresh from the garden.

'Come to help me, cuddies?' she said, stopping to address the raft of eider ducks waddling towards her. She smiled as their familiar cooing call resounded across the water, harmonising with the percussive susurration of the waves against the shore of Brownsman Island. It was the sound of her childhood.

Grace Darling had known from a young age that the secluded natural world of the Farne Islands was where she belonged. She was one of the few people ever to have lived on the Farnes. There had been monks and hermits intermittently through the centuries, and now there were the Darlings. Grace's family had moved to Brownsman when she was just three weeks old and, as the island's only inhabitants, she and her eight siblings had spent a very happy childhood playing with the resident seals and seabirds. Grace adored the puffins, guillemots and terns, and especially the eider ducks.

Despite having nine children to raise, Grace's mother Thomasin somehow also found time to rear animals and grow crops in the net-covered walled garden next to their tiny cottage attached to a lighthouse, where Grace's father was the proud keeper. It was William Darling's job to survey the surrounding waters for ships in distress. Fierce winds often battered the north-east coast and, over the years, many sailors had lost their lives trying and failing to navigate the hazardous outcrop of dolerite rocks that made up the Farne Islands.

The trouble was, Brownsman Light was too close to the mainland to reach the outermost isles, where the weather was the most perilous and the rocks the most rugged. So, when Grace was ten years old, Brownsman Light had been extinguished and the Darlings had relocated further out to sea, to a newly built, modern lighthouse on Longstone Rock.

That was twelve years ago, Grace marvelled. Impressive as Longstone Lighthouse was, she still missed living here, on Brownsman Island. The cottage was now rather weathered by the sea, but the garden remained intact and its soil, fertilised by an excess of guano from the local birdlife, teemed with rich vegetation. Nothing could grow on the bleak, barren Longstone Rock, so their old garden continued to be a vital food supply. Grace would regularly row over to Brownsman to revisit her childhood and gather their crops.

Grace was impressed with today's bountiful supply of spuds. She washed her muddy fingers in the sea, looked out at the vastness of the unbroken blue, reassembled her thick brown hair into a messy bun and dragged the potato-laden coble into the water. It was heavy work, but Grace's slender stature belied the strength of her strong and sturdy arms, which were well trained in rowing the distance between Brownsman and Longstone.

Grace knew these waters like the back of her hand. Although she had never been to school, she was well educated by her father, and seafaring was their most important subject. Grace was very knowledgeable about ships, weather patterns and currents. As she rowed, the cloud darkened and the sea started to swell. Grace picked up her pace.

By the time she reached Longstone, the weather had deteriorated. Under thick, dark clouds, an intimidating mist was rolling across the sea. Grace hauled the coble out of the water, which was becoming more volatile by the second, and onto the craggy terrain. She unloaded the potato sack, just as a huge wave roared in and broke over her. Shocked and soaked, Grace blinked away the water to see that the force of the receding wave was pulling the coble back out to sea.

She ran forwards, grabbing hold of the boat, and tugged it further inland.

A strong north-easterly wind was picking up as Grace struggled to wrestle the coble over to the boatshed. She needed an extra pair of hands; help from one of her parents. The lighthouse door swung open. Bundled in a shawl and apron, Thomasin Darling hitched up her plain pale-grey dress and hurried down the uneven stone steps as fast as her 64-year-old legs could carry her. William Darling, a sprightlier 52, was ahead of her, already helping Grace haul the coble into the boatshed.

These days, it was only Grace who still lived with her parents. Her seven siblings had all left home to find work or spouses on the mainland.

Grace found it lonely sometimes, but the seclusion suited her shyness. At 22 years of age, she felt it was her duty to stay with her ageing parents and help them with the upkeep of the lighthouse.

She looked up at it: a smart red-and-white circular tower, crowned with a revolving beacon. Complete with an adjoining boathouse and oil store, and standing almost 90 feet tall, it was a mighty fortress able to withstand any storm. It was Grace's home and sanctuary, and she retreated into it.

Grace sat by the wood stove to dry off and warm up while Mr Darling updated his logbook and Mrs Darling battened down the hatches.

Fear Death by Water

'Here you go, my angel,' said Mrs Darling, handing her daughter a hand-knitted blanket to snuggle under. 'There's some hot milk on the stove.'

'Thanks, Mam,' Grace replied, pouring herself a cup. She sipped gratefully.

'It's going to be a rough night,' said Mr Darling. 'This storm has arrived sooner than expected. I had better start preparing the light. I'll be up in the lantern room if you need me.'

William Darling's experience and reputation as a lighthouse keeper were second-to-none. Grace had always helped her mother with the housework and, now she was older, she shared some of her father's responsibilities too.

Lighthouse keeping was a full-time, two-person job. Every day, the brass reflectors had to be polished, the lamps and windows cleaned, the oil supply checked and the wicks trimmed to keep the oil burning. Every night, it was imperative that someone kept watch for ships as the light shone brightly from dusk till dawn.

Just before sunset, Grace wound her way up the steep spiral staircase to the top of the tower, to join her father. She stepped into the lantern room, taking in the 360-degree view of the North Sea. It never failed to impress her. How she loved the ocean. It made her feel small, but not in an insignificant way. Small because it always reminded her she was part of something bigger.

'The barometer needle has dropped,' reported Mr Darling. 'This storm will soon become a thunderstorm.'

'I'll light the beacon,' said Grace. This was her favourite job. She lit a candle, and then she used the candle to light the wicks. The wicks caught the flame, and a brilliant light filled the room. The beam shone fourteen miles out to sea. A good job too, because the sea and sky were pitch black tonight. Grace feared for the sailors when there was no moonlight.

A huge bolt of lightning shot through the sky.

'You'd better get some sleep while you can, Grace,' said Mr Darling.

As the thunder rumbled, Grace bade her father a goodnight and wound her way down to her bedroom. She hoped and prayed that there were no ships out at sea tonight.

Chapter Two
The Oncoming Storm

Why was there Artron energy on the Darlings' barometer? the Doctor wondered as he left the museum and stepped outside onto Radcliffe Road.

Why did the barometer react to my sonic?

What did Grace see in the ocean that terrified her so much?

The sun hit his face. A rare bliss in this region of Earth. It was a gorgeous summer's day in the quaint village of Bamburgh. In the distance, the broad North Sea kissed the horizon and just across the road stood St Aidan's Church: an unassuming, neat twelfth-century structure of squared stone, tinged with neutral pinks, yellows and whites. The western tower, standing on its chamfered plinth, rose in four stages of varying height, reaching up to the clear blue sky, which complemented the green of the grass in the graveyard below.

The Doctor crossed the road and entered the graveyard through a rusty old gate which sounded like it hadn't been oiled for centuries. He walked along the path that snaked its way through scattered headstones until he reached the Monument to Grace Darling.

He stalled for a moment at the Grade II listed Gothic shrine, looking at the effigy of Grace Darling recumbent on a stone mattress adorned with seaweed carvings, which lay under a three-arched canopy supported by metal colonnettes. A ghost of the past shivered through the Doctor's body. He shook it off and slid into the sleek, spacious control room of his TARDIS, which was parked just behind the memorial.

Music, he thought, heading straight for the jukebox. He lingered in front of the music machine, considering what he was in the mood for. He jabbed at the buttons. The distinctive opening riff of Stevie Wonder's 'Superstition' blasted through the speakers.

The Doctor closed his eyes and bobbed his head in time with the hi-hats. As the clavinet kicked in, he couldn't help himself: he grinned and broke into a groove. He'd spent so many of his lives carrying the weight of the world, but now, on the odd occasion, he was determined to allow himself to be carefree. It felt nice. It felt new. And boy, it felt good. In this particular body the Doctor found he enjoyed music more than ever before.

The roundel lights flashed rhythmically in different shades of blue. The Doctor shimmied his way around the console, fiddling with the controls in time with the beat and setting the coordinates for 7 September 1838, Longstone Rock, Northumberland, England, Earth. *That Artron energy reading on the Darlings' barometer was faint, but it was definitely there*, the Doctor thought. *Why?*

He was intrigued. And he could never resist the opportunity to meet a historical legend.

The Doctor pulled the lever.

His eyes twinkled as he watched the central time rotor chug up and down. He smiled, happy to be alive, and giddy with anticipation for another adventure. He would never get used to this.

All of a sudden, the console began flashing red.

'What now?' said the Doctor, switching off the music. 'Sorry, Stevie.'

He was quickly able to diagnose the problem: an almighty bolt of lightning, five times hotter than the sun, had struck his ship and the fluid link was overloading. The TARDIS jolted violently, tossing its pilot from side to side. The Doctor flailed about the console like a hyperactive spider on skates, trying to regain control of his ship, but it was going haywire, veering off course.

Seconds later, the TARDIS groaned to a standstill. The Doctor groaned too, as all light and life drained from the ship.

'No, no, no, no, no, no!'

The Doctor flicked switches and pressed buttons in a frantic attempt to resuscitate his vessel. But no luck. He kicked the console in a burst of frustration, then sniffed and licked the air. A metallic taste fizzed on his tongue, confirming his worst fears: the damaged fluid link was releasing vaporised mercury into the TARDIS.

'Not again,' said the Doctor in exasperation.

The fumes kept leaking. Before long, it would become toxic. There was no choice but to evacuate. The Doctor dashed for the door, released the latch and stepped outside.

Where have I landed? he wondered. He was certainly not on Longstone Rock. *How far have I veered off course?* It was the dead of night, but the glow of a few scattered lanterns provided just enough light to establish that he was on a ship: the deserted upper deck of a large paddle steamer. Bow side, to be precise. A tall single central funnel stood between two massive masts where two vast waxed canvas sails flapped noisily in the north-easterly gale-force wind. Torrential rain drummed on the deserted wooden decking.

The Doctor had been on deck for less than a minute but he was already soaked through. He looked around to find shelter, ideally somewhere that would give him a further clue as to exactly where he was and where he was headed. He was drawn towards the light radiating from the ship's paddle house across the deck. As he approached, he could see the shadowy figure of a middle-aged man at the helm.

'Captain?' said the Doctor, knocking on the window. No response. The Doctor knocked a little louder. 'Captain?'

The Doctor pressed his face up to the glass. *What's he playing at?*

Not only was the captain not listening, he wasn't looking either. He was clutching the ship's steering wheel, navigating with his eyes held tightly shut. The Doctor pushed open the door into the paddle house.

'Captain,' he said again, determined to get a response this time. 'Is everything okay in here?'

'This storm is an omen,' the captain trembled.

'What makes you say that?'

'I saw something in the waves.'

'What did you see? Describe it to me.'

The captain shook his head.

'Look, I'm sure you know how to sail with your eyes closed, but it's not such a good idea, you know,' said the Doctor, grabbing hold of the wheel to help steady the captain's trembling arms. He evaluated the man's face and frowned. 'Can you open your eyes?'

'They're burning.'

'Let me see.'

'Who are you?'

'You'll find out if you open your eyes.' The captain shook his head again. 'I'm a Doctor. Come on, open your eyes for me, Captain.'

'I can't see it again. I can't.'

'There's nothing to see,' said the Doctor reassuringly. 'Seriously, it's pitch dark out there. Whatever it was you saw, it's gone now. I promise you.'

Tentatively the captain did as he was told and the Doctor peered into his eyes. They were wide with terror. The whites of his eyes were bloodshot and his pupils were extremely dilated.

'How's your vision? Can you see? How many fingers am I holding up?'

'Two eyes,' said the captain.

'Close. Two *fingers*.'

'I saw two eyes. Burning. And now my eyes are burning. My *mind* is burning.' The captain clutched his head in agony.

The Doctor scanned the man's eyes with his sonic screwdriver. 'Hmm...' He frowned; the sonic was picking up some sort of psychic spoor. A mark left by a wild animal. Except it wasn't a physical marking; it was imprinted inside the captain's mind. And, clearly, that mind was struggling to handle it.

The Doctor slipped the sonic back into his pocket. He felt the letter he had taken from the museum. He remembered the words Grace had written: *the most terrifying vision – the blazing eyes of a beast in the ocean.*

'Okay,' said the Doctor, staring into the blackness in front of them. 'I see no ships. I see no eyes.' *But I do see a revolving light in the distance.* The Doctor scanned over the ship's navigation charts on the captain's desk. *We're crossing the North Sea. The ship's set off from Hull and is heading for Dundee.*

Just then, another man entered the paddle house, the tail of his raincoat flapping in the wind. He was holding a lantern and he looked concerned.

He looked at the Doctor. 'Who are you?'

The Doctor flashed his psychic paper. 'Ship's doctor.'

Fear Death by Water

Then the man looked at the captain, quivering at the helm. 'Captain Humble, are you quite all right?'

'I'm on the case,' said the Doctor, 'don't worry.'

'I'm afraid there is great reason to worry, sir.'

'What is it now, Chief Engineer?' asked the captain.

'Captain, the third boiler has also failed. The engines won't respond. Effectively, we are at sea with no power.'

The Doctor absorbed the news. The light from the chief engineer's lantern illuminated the grave fear etched onto the captain's weather-worn face.

The waves roared. The wind howled.

'Gusts are fifty knots and rising,' said the chief engineer. 'We are sure to blow off course. This storm is not going away any time soon.'

'As I said,' replied the captain, as more thunder rumbled. 'This storm is an omen. A beast is rising from the deep. The ocean will consume us all. Fear death by water.' He took off his hat.

'What are you doing?' asked the Doctor.

'I am the drowned sailor.'

'No,' said the Doctor, shaking his head. 'You're the *captain*. You're alive. And all the time you're alive, you can't give up. You have a duty. How many passengers are on board this ship?'

'Sixty-three.'

'Sixty-three souls in need of their captain.'

'There's no hope for them. No hope for any of us.'

'There's *always* hope.'

The captain passed his skipper's cap to the Doctor. 'Take this. If you think there's any hope of saving this ship, then I leave that to you. Skipper.' He began to walk out of the paddle house.

'Where are you going?'

'To the cabins,' replied the captain. 'If I am to drown, I would prefer to do so with my wife by my side.'

'Captain!' the Doctor called after him. 'Get back here! I am not the commander of this ship. This is *your* ship!'

The captain ignored the Doctor and continued to walk away, to embrace his fate.

'Follow him, could you?' said the Doctor to the chief engineer, as he hurried over to man the abandoned helm.

The Doctor held the captain's hat in his hands. *So much for not interfering,* he thought. *I can't wear this.* Instead he took hold of the wheel with one hand, then picked up the captain's telescope with the other and squinted through the glass at the nocturnal horizon.

They were closer to the lighthouse now, about a mile off. As its beam swept across the sea, it illuminated a jagged black shadow looming in front of them.

The chief engineer was right.

The ship had blown off course.

We're heading straight for the rocks!

Chapter Three
In the Cold Light of Night

Grace couldn't sleep. Rain lashed at her bedroom window, which rattled in the howling gale. She used to share this room with her sister Betsy, but the stormy nights were scarier now that she slept alone. She could hear the huge waves crashing against the base of the lighthouse, which, at high tide, was fully exposed to the fury of the North Sea.

Thankfully, her bedroom was on the third floor of Longstone Lighthouse. Flooding had been an unfortunately frequent occurrence in her downstairs bedroom at their old lighthouse on Brownsman Island. The windows often failed to withstand storms, meaning large waves would cascade through the broken frames and shattered glass. On one occasion, when she was a young girl, Grace came close to drowning as the room filled with seawater and forced the door shut. The memory of it still sent shivers down her spine with every subsequent storm that passed.

Nevertheless, tonight, Grace braved sitting by the window, diligently checking her telescope. It was a good vantage point, probably the second best after the lantern room. On such a cloudy, starless night as this, nothing could be seen properly without the lighthouse's beam. As the beacon revolved, light swept across the sea, illuminating the Farne Island rocks for a split second every thirty seconds.

In this fleeting window of light, Grace surveyed the sea for ships.

The hours passed slowly and the storm raged on.

Grace checked the time. It was half past four in the morning. High tide.

Fifteen minutes later, a dark shape out in the inky sea caught Grace's eye. She squinted. Her heart thumped in her chest. She hared downstairs.

'Father!' she cried, bursting into his bedroom and stirring him from his sleep. 'I can see a ship, I'm certain of it! It's about a mile away, looks like it's struck Big Harcar Rock.'

'Show me,' said Mr Darling, getting up immediately.

They hurried up the steep spiral stairs in silence. Reaching the lantern room, Grace aligned the telescope towards the rocks and anxiously waited for her father's review. Mr Darling watched for several rotations before he confirmed Grace's fear.

'Good heavens!' said Mr Darling. 'You're quite right, Grace.'

A ship had crashed. And it was heeling over.

'What can we do to help?' asked Grace. 'Are there any survivors?'

Fear Death by Water

'No way to tell,' said Mr Darling, still pressing the telescope against his eye. 'Visibility is poor, and the sea's very rough. It's much too dangerous to do anything now. We must keep checking the glass and reassess the situation at first light once the tide has fallen.'

Chapter Four
Rocky Horror Show

The Doctor tensed in helpless horror as jagged rock tore into the bow of the paddle steamer. A harrowing crunch brought the vessel to a standstill. And its captain was nowhere to be seen.

Where is the first mate? thought the Doctor. *Who is the first mate?*

There was no time to find out.

The Doctor ran across the upper deck, almost slipping on the large puddles on the floor as rain pelted into his face, obscuring his vision. *I need to find the ship's bell.* He wiped the water out of his eyes. *There!* He darted over to the bell. The vessel's name was engraved on the brass: SS *Forfarshire*.

The Doctor's blood ran cold. The TARDIS hadn't veered too far off course after all. That rotating light he could see was coming from Longstone Rock. And this was the *Forfarshire* on the night it would perish.

I shouldn't be here, the Doctor told himself. *I should leave. I should find a barometer, source ten millimetres of mercury to refuel the TARDIS's fluid link and get off this sinking ship as quickly as is Time Lordly possible.*

Shouldn't I?

A pang of guilt flooded through the Doctor. There were 63 passengers and crew below deck, the majority destined to drown. He knew he shouldn't interfere with established events. This was a fixed point in time. A historical moment that needed to happen.

Was he really going to leave the people on this ship with no captain?

No way.

The Doctor sounded the bell. Its metallic ringing echoed through the night, clashing with the howl of the storm to create a cacophony of noise. It wasn't long before terrified passengers began to assemble on the upper deck, woken from their sweet slumber into the beginnings of a nightmare.

'What's happening?' a passenger cried.

'We've stopped moving!' cried another.

'Where's the captain?'

'Are we going to drown?'

'Make your way up to the deck as calmly as you can,' the Doctor shouted as he continued to sound the alarm. *Where are the lifeboats?* he wondered.

All of a sudden, a strong gust of wind caught the bow-side sail and the ship lurched, flinging everyone sideways.

'Whoa!' the Doctor exclaimed, letting go of the bell and grabbing hold of the nearest railing to steady his footing. A swell of sea scooped the *Forfarshire* back into its clutches, releasing it from the rock's hold. The vessel floundered in the ocean, then, with another grinding blow, smashed bow-first back into the rock, mounting the dolerite once again. But, this time, the impact was too much.

The *Forfarshire* fell into a stunned, anxious silence. The Doctor could hear the midship timbers creaking ominously.

'BOW!' he shouted. 'GET TO THE FRONT OF THE SHIP! NOW!'

The creaking got louder, until the timbers were splintering, and then the entire ship started splitting in two.

The *Forfarshire* descended into chaos. The thirty or so passengers who had made it from their cabins to the upper deck collided with one another, panicking, crying, confused, disoriented, as they attempted to follow the Doctor's instruction, struggling up the slippery deck towards the half of the ship that was held secure against the rock. Seawater gushed into the hold through the shattered hull and the ship's back section was tilting further towards the sea.

The Doctor looked over the bow's edge at the rock below, assessing the best route down. It was going to be tricky – it was a twenty-foot drop – but it was the only way off this sinking ship. Plucking his sonic screwdriver from his pocket, the Doctor zapped a length of rope to detach it from the damaged front mast, which was wobbling precariously in the gale.

He tied one end around the railing in a tight constrictor knot and tossed the other end overboard. It hit the rock's algae-covered surface. It was exactly the right length. *Still got it*, thought the Doctor.

'Climb down to the rock,' he shouted. 'Use the rope. Abseil!'

But the passengers weren't listening. They were too distressed by the sound of the screams for help that were coming from the other end of the ship. Those who had failed to make it across to the bow side were now hanging off the stern's broken railings with freezing cold fingers. They held on helplessly, wailing and shouting until they fell to their deaths, soul after soul after soul claimed by the icy North Sea.

The stern was sinking fast. There was now very little timber keeping it attached to the bow. The Doctor locked eyes with a young boy – no more than seven years old by the look of it – holding on for dear life.

'HOLD ON!' the Doctor yelled. He detached a second length of rope from the mast and tied it around another nearby railing. Then he took his intelligent gloves out of his pockets, slipped them on, grabbed hold of the other end of the rope and launched himself into a slippery skid: down the soaked slope of the foredeck, sliding like an Olympic skier, propelled by the rush of wind and the torrent of rain, coasting, faster, faster, faster. The Doctor's hero instinct surged, an uncontainable wave of swashbuckling energy as he steeled himself to —

Fear Death by Water

JUMP!

The Doctor flew over the gaping crevasse between the bow and the stern, his coattails billowing behind him. He landed on the other side, now sliding down the stern, still clutching the rope, rope-burn free, thanks to the gloves.

The stern wobbled as the rope tugged taut, abruptly breaking the Doctor's momentum just as he reached the little boy at the railings.

'I've got you,' said the Doctor, catching his breath. He pulled the boy close to the front of his body and held him tightly as he tied the end of the rope around both their waists, binding them together.

'You can let go now!' But the boy's bony fingers were frozen around the railing in a claw-like shape, too stiff to move. The Doctor gently prised them off the metal bar then reached around the child, firmly grasped the stretch of rope with both gloved hands and began to climb back up the steep slope of the stern towards the secure bow end of the ship.

His mavity-resistant gloves sped up the ascent, but the Doctor knew he was fast running out of time. The stern wouldn't hold out for much longer.

As he reached the precipice of the crevasse, *THUD!* Both halves of the fractured *Forfarshire* juddered as the front mast toppled down, narrowly missing the TARDIS, but giving the stern the last nudge it needed to give way. The Doctor could feel the hull shifting as it shook, on the brink of collapse.

'On three, we jump. Okay?'

The boy nodded.

'One! Two! THREE!'

It was perilously close. They landed on the bow as the stern finally broke away to become a separate vessel, engulfed by the sea. The funnel and paddles, the engine room, the cargo hold, all the cabins, furniture, suitcases and passengers alike disgorged into the ocean.

The Doctor sighed, in sorrow, in relief. How many people had drowned, along with the captain, he wondered. Thirty? Forty?

More?

Focus, Doctor.

Around a dozen passengers stranded on the upper foredeck were desperately clutching onto one another as wave upon wave thrashed over the remains of the *Forfarshire*, which clung stubbornly onto the rock.

'What's your name?' the Doctor asked the little boy who had attached himself to his leg like a limpet.

'James!' shouted a woman, running over and hugging her son. Then she grabbed the Doctor by the arm. 'Please help! It's my daughter.'

'Where is she?' He followed the woman over to the small girl. She had a bloody bruise on her forehead and was lying on the deck unconscious. James tried to shake her awake.

'Careful,' said the Doctor, pulling him off. 'What happened?'

Fear Death by Water

'The mast hit her,' said the woman, sobbing into her daughter's chest. 'Her head. Oh, Matilda. My poor Matilda.'

James and Matilda. The Doctor registered the names. He'd read them in the museum.

He checked Matilda's pulse. She didn't have one.

'Listen to me, my sweets.' The Doctor spoke as calmly as he could. 'I need you both to let go of her, just for a minute, is that okay?' The Doctor placed the heel of his hand in the centre of her chest and pressed down smoothly and firmly at a rate of two pumps per second. *Pump pump.*

'What are you doing?' asked James.

'Keeping –' *pump pump* – 'her –' *pump pump* – 'alive,' replied the Doctor.

Matilda stirred. She coughed and sputtered and gasped for air as her mother pulled her into a tight embrace. 'My darling!' she sobbed. Then she pulled in James and hugged both her children as close as she could. 'Oh, my darlings!'

The Doctor watched this family of three, blinking away tears. He knew that tonight was the night these children were supposed to die. And he had just saved them. His stomach heaved. So did the bow.

Pull yourself together, Doctor.

He glanced at his TARDIS. He had a thought: the simplest solution.

No. He rejected the idea. They shouldn't take shelter in the TARDIS.

They couldn't.

They had to get down to the rock, otherwise Grace Darling wouldn't see any survivors and her story wouldn't be history. He had already meddled enough.

'Come on!' said the Doctor. He helped James and Matilda and their mother to their feet. 'We need to get onto the rock!'

But once they had done so, the Doctor knew there was nothing more he could do. For the sake of history, he couldn't rescue this young family, or any of the other survivors, from the rock.

There was, however, someone else who could…

Chapter Five
The Ship's Graveyard

Grace Darling sat at her bedroom window in Longstone Lighthouse checking her telescope until the break of dawn. Then—

'Father!' she exclaimed. 'FATHER!'

Mr Darling came running into Grace's room. 'What is it?'

'There are people on the Big Harcar Rock!' she said, passing him her telescope. 'I can see them. At least four, perhaps more. Look!'

'So there are,' said Mr Darling.

BOOM! The sound of a nine-pounder gun, fired from the ramparts of Bamburgh Castle. It was a signal to the survivors that they had been spotted by onlookers patrolling the coast.

Grace knew the protocol: at this very moment the castle's governor would be preparing to embark on the three-mile journey from Bamburgh to the village of Seahouses to alert the lifeboatmen at the harbour.

'Will Seahouses manage to send a lifeboat?' she asked. There was some hazy daylight now, and the tide was lower, but the storm had not subsided.

Mr Darling stood next to Grace and looked out the window. He shook his head.

'No lifeboats could be launched from Seahouses in this weather. Even if they could, they're five miles off. They'd not get there in time.' He paused, his jaw clenching. 'I'll have to go.'

'I shall go with you,' Grace said.

'No,' snapped her father. 'This storm is as fierce as any I have ever seen. It will take all our strength, and our small coble might not make it—'

'If it was one of my brothers standing before you now,' said Grace, 'you wouldn't hesitate in taking them with you.'

'You could lose your life, Grace.'

Grace nodded. 'I know.' Fear filled her stomach like a lead weight, but she knew it was her father's duty to save the people on Big Harcar Rock if he could. And she felt it was her duty to help him.

'We should get started, Father,' she said.

'You're quite determined to do this, aren't you?' said Mrs Darling, wrapping a thick woollen shawl around Grace's shoulders and winding a long hand-knitted scarf around her neck.

'There are people out there relying upon us.'

Mr and Mrs Darling looked at their daughter. Grace read the mixture of pride and trepidation on their faces. She hugged her mother reassuringly tight.

Fear Death by Water

'I love you, Mam,' she whispered.

'I love you too, my angel,' Mrs Darling whispered back. Then she embraced her husband, who looked every bit the dashing hero in his old navy-blue keeper's coat, complete with shiny brass buttons and dark seaman trousers.

'Keep her safe, William,' she begged.

William nodded. 'Are you ready, Grace?'

She was as ready as she would ever be.

Grace stepped out of the safety of the lighthouse and into the treacherous wind and rain. Their violence shocked her into a state of high alert. She was tired – she hadn't slept a wink last night – but adrenalin was filling her entire body.

She helped her father untether the coble from the boatshed, trying her best to hide her nerves, to prove to him that she was every bit as capable as any one of her brothers.

'We must stay south of the rocks,' Mr Darling instructed, as they carried their boat down to the water. 'It's not the direct course, but will give us some shelter from the currents.'

They pushed the coble into the choppy water. Her mother and father did their best to hold it steady as Grace climbed aboard. It was hard to keep her balance. Their boat was a sturdy little thing, but it was designed for a minimum crew of three strong men. Grace said a short, silent prayer for protection as her father took his position next to her.

'Godspeed!' called Mrs Darling, waving them off from the doorway with a handkerchief already damp with tears.

They were at the mercy of the ocean now.

Waves broke ferociously against the coble. Grace and her father held an oar each, but to begin with they mostly let the wind and the tide carry them south through the stretch of water known as Craford's Gut, until they reached their turning point.

'We need to row west!' shouted Mr Darling.

Grace could barely hear him over the roar of the wind and waves, but followed his action instinctively. She clasped her oar with both hands, pushed off with her legs and pulled with all the strength of her upper body, trying to keep in time with her father's rhythm.

Row. Row. Row.

The North Sea was monstrous. Wild waves towered like dark grey mountains; it was impossible to see above or beyond them. Each one caught the coble, swept it up and held it on the high crest before throwing it back down into the trough of the next wave.

Grace held on grimly but was almost tossed out into the water. Before she could catch her breath, up they swept and down they plunged. Up and down, over and over again.

Suddenly, a flare of bright light from about fifty yards away half-blinded Grace. Sharp pain shot through her temples, scorching the back of her eyes. She blinked hard to reset her vision, but the image didn't fade.

Fear Death by Water

Through a huge wave, an enormous pair of eyes were glaring at her. The eyes were angry. Bestial. They were yellow, with flashes of red, as though they were on fire.

Fear seared Grace's heart. However much she wanted to look away, she couldn't. She was transfixed. Caught in this creature's tormenting gaze. Until...

The coble came crashing back down with the wave and seawater flooded over the sides. Grace was drenched to the bone and shaken to her core. She searched the sea, but the mysterious eyes had vanished just as quickly as they had appeared.

'Father!' she called.

'Are you quite all right, Grace?' asked Mr Darling.

'Did you see that, Father?'

'See what?' asked Mr Darling, blinking sea spray out of his eyes.

'Fire in the waves!'

'There's no fire, Grace. It's water. Wretched waves. This spindrift is certainly messing with my vision. Come on, keep rowing. You're doing so well.'

Grace kept rowing. But she couldn't get the image of the eyes out of her mind. It was burning, making her head ache, as well as her arms.

Focus, Grace! Row. Row. Row.

She was seriously tiring now. With every stroke she worried she wouldn't have enough strength for the next. But at long last, Big Harcar Rock emerged into view through the mist.

'Help! HELP! Help us!'

Hearing desperate cries, Grace rowed vigorously. Her oar hit against something hard in the water: it was a plank of wood. Then another. And another. Then a suitcase. And a chair. Debris swamped the sea.

It was a sight Grace would never forget as long as she lived. Crashed into the rock ahead was what remained of a large modern paddle steamer. The stern was nowhere to be seen and the bow was fixed fast on the rock. Dozens of dead bodies were floating face down in the water.

Think about the people who are still alive, she told herself, horrified. Twelve survivors were waving and shouting on the rock. She could see them now.

They rowed as close to Big Harcar as they dared, then Mr Darling passed Grace his oar.

'Grace, it's all down to you now. I need you to keep the coble in a steady position right next to the rock so people can climb in. The waves will fight back, but I know you can do this. I believe in you.'

Grace steeled herself and nodded. 'And I you, Father. Be safe.'

Mr Darling sprang onto the rock, leaving Grace to manage the coble alone.

And so she did. She rowed – back and forth, back and forth, back and forth, always careful not to hit the corpses with her oar. She knew that if she lost control, even for a moment, the boat would be smashed to smithereens, stranding them all. Everyone's lives were in her hands.

Fear Death by Water

Her numb, cramped, frozen hands. Her eyes stung with salty sea spray. Her muscles ached excruciatingly. Her entire body was shattered. How much did she have left in her? She didn't know.

'KEEP GOING, GRACE!' Mr Darling bellowed from the rock.

Determined not to let her father down, Grace pushed through the pain. Out of the corner of her eye, she could just make out the commotion on the rock, of her father prioritising the passengers as quickly as he could.

A young woman collapsed into the coble first, accompanied by two small children. Grace ignored her impulse to stop to comfort them and kept rowing, like a machine, keeping the coble steady so that a young man with a damaged leg could clamber in next. He was moved to tears at the sight of Grace rowing, risking her life for the sake of theirs. Another injured man followed. The coble was getting heavy now but Grace didn't waver for a single second, though her strength was dwindling. One more man embarked: the strongest and fittest of the survivors, strategically selected by Mr Darling. He sat next to Grace, wrapped his orange leather trench coat around her shoulders then took control of the oars.

Relief. Profound relief flooded through Grace's veins.

'You, young lady, are *amazing*!' said the strong man. He rowed effortlessly. '*Beyond* amazing! Are you okay?'

Grace felt she might pass out with exhaustion. 'I'm fine,' she lied. 'Thank you for rowing, sir.'

'Not a sir. Just call me the Doctor.'
'You're a physician?'
'And you are...'
'Grace Darling.'
'Of course you are!' exclaimed the Doctor. 'Grace Darling! Dazzling name, Grace Darling! It's a thrill to meet you. At last.'

What did he mean, at last? thought Grace. *Why was this man so excited to see her?* Granted, she had just saved his life, but these were unusually high spirits for a man who'd just survived a shipwreck. She decided not to dwell on it. Besides, she was grateful for his energy and thought how good it would be to have a physician on board. Some of the survivors were in the most terrible state. Grace was particularly concerned for the poor children and their mother. She moved further down the hull to sit beside them.

'There's no more room in the boat,' Grace heard her father explain to the remaining men on the rock. 'But we will come back for you as quickly as we can, you have my word.'

Mr Darling hopped back into the coble, which rocked with the unbalanced weight of so many passengers, but the Doctor kept control of the boat.

'Thank you, sir,' said Mr Darling, taking back one of the oars. 'I shall need your help rowing back for a second journey to rescue the remaining men, if you'd be so kind as to oblige?'

'Aye aye, skipper,' said the Doctor.

'The lassie did a good job,' said the survivor with the injured leg.

'That's my daughter,' Mr Darling replied, beaming at Grace with pride as she transferred the Doctor's coat to the traumatised young mother.

'What's your name?' Grace asked her.

'Sarah Dawson.'

'And are these your children?'

Sarah nodded.

'They're lovely. What are their names?'

'James and Matilda.'

Grace gave Sarah's shoulders a comforting rub and smiled reassuringly at the children. 'We will be safe and dry soon, I promise. The worst is over.'

Chapter Six
John Smith and the Common Men

'Come in, come in, come in,' said Mrs Darling, welcoming the Doctor through the front door of Longstone Lighthouse. He had just returned from Big Harcar with Mr Darling, having rescued the remaining survivors from the rock. 'Come in and get yourself warm. Grace will give you a blanket.'

The lighthouse was cosy, the Doctor thought, if a tad smaller on the inside. Probably because there were so many unexpected guests. The eleven survivors were squeezed inside the circular room on the ground floor, which was a kitchen, dining room and living area all in one.

Although the space was full of people, a silent grief filled the room.

'As you can see,' said Mrs Darling, 'we are a little cramped here now, but please make yourself at home. Doctor... what was it?'

'Smith,' the Doctor found himself saying. 'John Smith.' *Why not? For old time's sake.*

'Find yourself somewhere to sit, Doctor Smith. You must be exhausted.'

On the contrary. He was buzzing, unlike the other survivors, who looked bone-weary. *Poor humans*, the Doctor thought. What a disadvantage it must be to have the energy supply of an earthling.

He smiled at Grace, who was handing out warm knitted blankets to the latest arrivals on the other side of the room.

'You have a phenomenal daughter, Mrs D,' the Doctor said quietly, 'do you know that?'

'Course I do,' said Mrs Darling with flushed cheeks. 'I'm her mother.'

'I'm amazed she managed such a feat,' said Mr Darling, entering the room and shaking himself dry, having shut the coble safely away in the boatshed.

'I'm not,' said Mrs Darling. 'She's tougher than she looks, that girl. She takes after you, you know.'

'Poor lass.'

Mrs Darling pecked her husband on the cheek. 'Thank you for bringing her back home to me, William.'

'I promised I would.' Mr Darling turned to the Doctor and held out his hand. 'Please let me shake you by the hand and thank you for your assistance, sir. I couldn't have returned to the rock without you. Now, if you'll excuse me, I must attend to the light.'

'You must eat something too, William. I'll bring you up a bowl of soup. Good heavens, it must be boiling over by now,' said Mrs Darling, wiping her hands on her pinny as she hurried over to the wood stove.

'Would you like a blanket?' asked Grace, appearing at the Doctor's side.

'I'm fine without, thanks,' replied the Doctor.

'Come and sit down at least,' said Grace. 'You should really rest.'

'A doctor is never off duty. Put me to work.'

'If you are sure…'

'Sure I'm sure.'

'Then could you possibly take a look at Sarah Dawson's daughter?' Grace asked. 'She has a head wound that needs tending to.'

'I'll need bandages. And a clean damp cloth,' said the Doctor.

Grace nodded then hurried off to find the medical supplies.

Sarah Dawson was sitting in a rocking chair, clutching James and Matilda either side of her She was swinging back and forth to keep them asleep.

The Doctor crouched down at Sarah's side. 'How're you doing?' He could see that she was too shattered to respond. 'How're *they* doing? Can I…?'

He reached a hand towards Matilda's head, gently sweeping her hair aside so he could examine the injury underneath.

As he did so, Matilda stirred.

'Hey, my sweet,' he said softly. 'Quite an impressive bump you've got here. Can I take a look at it?' Matilda nodded. 'You're very brave,' he told her.

Upon close inspection, it didn't look like the skull was fractured so, once Grace returned with the cloth, he applied pressure to the wound, then cleaned it up before winding a bandage around Matilda's forehead.

'Will she be all right?' Sarah asked anxiously.

The Doctor smiled sadly. More than anything, he wanted to say yes. He was relieved to see Matilda and her brother James were safe and sound for now. Deep down, however, he knew the prognosis wasn't good.

He had saved them but they shouldn't have survived. They were living on borrowed time.

And at some point, the universe would inevitably correct itself.

'I hope so,' the Doctor said.

He tried to blink away his tears before Sarah saw them.

'Ouch!' said James Kellie, as the Doctor fixed a dressing around his bloody leg.

'I'm so sorry,' said the Doctor, readjusting the knot on the bandage.

'Dinnae be silly. Better tae be alive wi' a gammy shank than nae to be alive at all. Besides, it's na fault o' yers, Doctor.'

'No,' snapped the man sitting next to James Kellie. 'It's the captain's!' It was the first time Daniel Donovan had spoken since the Doctor arrived. There was anger in his thick Irish accent. 'I told the captain we should turn back.'

'What happened?' asked Grace. Everyone's attention turned to Daniel, as though they had been waiting for a cue to discuss the tragedy.

'Two nights ago, we set off from Hull for Dundee,' Daniel explained. 'The first boiler started leaking that very same evening. I was a passenger on board, but I'm a ship's fireman, you see, so I knew something weren't right. I told the captain to terminate the voyage. But he was a proud man, Captain Humble. Never was a name less apt. He wouldn't listen, refused to turn back. Next night, the second boiler stopped working. Then the storm blew in. Our fool of a captain hoisted the sails and sailed right into the rocks.' Daniel placed his head in his hands. 'Within fifteen minutes, the *Forfarshire* had smashed clean in two.'

'That's when I saw you,' said Grace.

'We'd be dead without ye, for sure, lassie,' said James Kellie. 'What ye did oot there for us... why, 'twas th' most selfless act o' bravery I hae ever witnessed. We owe ye'n' yer father oor lives.'

'You owe us nothing at all,' said Grace.

The Doctor listened carefully to Daniel Donovan's account, hoping to glean from it any further clue as to what had happened to the captain in the paddle house just before he had arrived.

What was it the captain had seen in the waves?

'A beast is rising from the deep,' he had said.

'The ocean will consume us all.'

'Here,' said Mrs Darling, bustling around the room with bowls of hot potato soup in an attempt to defrost everyone's frozen cores and restore their crushed spirits. 'Get this down you. It'll be good for your souls.'

She handed bowls to Sarah and the children first. Then she served the male passengers – Daniel Donovan, James Kellie and Thomas Buchanan – next, followed by the five sole surviving *Forfarshire* crewmen, who all happened to be called John.

'We won't be forgetting your names in a hurry, will we?' said Mrs Darling, serving John MacQueen, the ship's coal trimmer, then the carpenter John Tulloch, followed by John Kidd and John Nicholson, the ship's firemen, and finally Jonathan Tickett, the ship's cook.

'I hope this is up to your usual standards,' said Mrs Darling.

'Ta, Ma'am,' Jonathan replied. 'Smells delicious.'

The Johns slurped hungrily and messily. *And I guess, just now, I'm one of them*, the Doctor thought, receiving his own bowl of soup from Mrs Darling with a smile.

He had such a soft spot for this planet, and on occasions such as this he was reminded why. Right here and now, in Victorian Northumberland, he was living through a story – a *legend* – that would be written about for centuries to come. The Doctor felt a swell of admiration in his hearts for the ambassadors of the human race sitting before him. Ordinary, humble human beings in an extraordinary situation. Rallying round one another. Saving each other.

Fear Death by Water

In their short, painful lives, it was humans like these who showed the Doctor a better way to live. Perhaps, sometimes, the human race helped him more than he helped them.

Chapter Seven
The Mind's Eye

Later that afternoon, the survivors, full of potato soup and cocoa, dozed in the living area.

Always too restless to sleep, the Doctor wound his way up the spiral staircase to the top of the lighthouse tower to join Grace, who had taken over from her father keeping watch.

'Knock, knock,' he said, sweeping into the lantern room.

'Hello, Doctor,' said Grace, lowering her telescope.

'Don't you ever stop?' the Doctor asked.

'Don't you? We must be extra vigilant in this weather,' said Grace. The storm had still shown no sign of subsiding.

'Twelve Argand oil lamps, surrounded by brass parabolic reflectors mounted onto a clockwork platform,' said the Doctor, admiring the technology in the room. 'Cutting edge. For its time. This is one of the first revolving lights in Great Britain, am I right?'

'Right!' said Grace. 'Would you like to light it?'

The Doctor grinned. 'I would *love* to light it.'

'Here,' said Grace, passing the Doctor a candle. 'Light the base of the wick.'

As the wick burst into flame, filling the lantern room with light, the Doctor beamed. 'I should visit lighthouses more often. Hey, I should *have* a lighthouse. Why don't I have a lighthouse?'

'They're high maintenance,' said Grace.

'So am I.'

Grace chuckled, then returned her attention to the telescope. The Doctor took the opportunity to nose around the lantern room. He spotted a familiar object on the side: Mr Darling's barometer. He glanced over his shoulder to check Grace was still distracted. She was. So he retrieved his sonic screwdriver from his pocket and scanned the instrument.

Déjà vu! He had already scanned it, of course, back in Grace's museum. Well, back in the future. *That must be why it reacted*, he realised. *Because I'm sonicking it* now; *162 years earlier.* There was no reading of Artron energy yet. And then another thought hit him. He needed mercury. This was his key to resuscitating the TARDIS. He went to pick up the barometer.

'What are you doing?' asked Grace.

'Oh,' said the Doctor, 'just admiring your barometer.'

She frowned. 'Why?'

'I'm a big fan of... instruments.'

'I suppose you are a man of science.' Grace picked up her telescope again.

'See anything?' said the Doctor, coming to stand next to her.

'No,' she replied. 'Thank goodness.'

'Hey, what did the ocean say to the lighthouse?' the Doctor asked.

'What did it *say*?'

'Nothing,' the Doctor grinned. 'It just waved.'

Grace couldn't help but laugh, then she flinched in pain.

'Joke that bad?' said the Doctor. 'I think it was invented around now...'

'Forgive me...' Grace cupped her hands around her head in agony.

'Oh, you're actually seriously in pain,' said the Doctor, hurrying to her side. 'What is it? What's wrong?'

'Nothing,' Grace replied, massaging her temples.

'You have a questionable definition of nothing.'

'I'm tired, that's all.'

'Then you should go to bed. Doctor's orders. Go on. I'll keep watch.'

'Sarah Dawson and the children are in my bed,' said Grace. 'Besides, I can't sleep. All I can think about is all those dead people I saw in the water.'

'I know the feeling,' said the Doctor.

Grace shook her head in despair. 'I have never thought about death so much as today. In truth, Doctor, I feel quite shaken. I was so scared out there.'

'Oh honey, that's okay,' said the Doctor. 'That fear was your superpower. That's what someone once told me. Just imagine, all that fear pumping through your veins while you were out there, rowing for your life. That fear made you stronger. Faster. It made you kinder. You didn't run away. You plucked up your courage and you rowed towards danger. Think of all those people asleep downstairs; they're alive right now, because of you.'

'Am I supposed to feel good about that?' asked Grace.

The Doctor didn't know what to say. Because if he was honest with himself, there was a part of him that got a kick out of danger, a thrill out of saving lives. At some point during his centuries travelling he had become the 'hero'. Or rather, the 'hero' had become him. Now, who would he be without it? It gave him his sense of purpose; his *modus operandi*. And he liked it.

'You did an incredible thing,' said the Doctor, blotting out his innermost thoughts. 'A very brave thing. But bravery comes at a cost. It's not easy.'

'I feel so terribly guilty. If only we had left for the rock earlier…'

The Doctor recognised the remorse on Grace's face. 'You don't always get to save everyone,' he said softly.

'I suppose you've had experience saving lives, in your occupation.'

'Saving lives… and losing them.'

'You're right, life and death come together,' said Grace. She screwed her eyes closed in pain, though the Doctor could see she was trying to suppress it.

'Right,' he said, putting his hands on her shoulders and turning her to face him. 'Come on, what's all this about?'

'It's a headache,' Grace replied, rubbing her eyes.

'Grace, honey. A *headache*? Really?'

She avoided eye contact.

'Look at me. Talk to me.'

Grace sighed, relenting, trying to search for the right words. 'While I was out in the coble, in the storm, I saw… something.'

The Doctor leant in closer, curious. 'What was it?'

'It sounds scarcely credible, but…' Grace looked into the Doctor's eyes. 'I saw a pair of eyes.'

'Blazing eyes?'

'How did you know?' asked Grace. 'Have you seen them too?'

'No. Go on,' said the Doctor. 'What did they look like?'

'They were bestial. Enormous. And they were on fire. They were looking right at me. *Into* me. I felt their fire. It felt like… an evil spirit.' Grace turned away, embarrased. 'I know it sounds impossible…'

'Not to me. Have you told anyone else?'

Grace shook her head. 'My father said he didn't see anything. He thinks I had sea spray in my eye. Or that I was hallucinating. Perhaps I was…'

The Doctor was well aware that stories of sea monsters had existed in primitive places by the sea throughout time. Often it was simply superstitious nonsense.

Often. But not always.

'I don't think you're hallucinating. I think the captain saw it too.'

'The captain?'

'On the *Forfarshire*.'

'So I am not mad or mistaken?' said Grace. 'I thought at first that my mind must have been playing tricks on me. But I know what I saw. And now that monster in the ocean is inside my mind.'

The Doctor looked deep into Grace's brown eyes and could see that she was terrified, though she was holding things together far better than poor old Captain Humble had managed.

'You say this monster you saw is inside your mind?'

Grace nodded. 'I still see those fire-eyes staring into the darkness of my mind's eye. It's been tormenting me all day.'

The Doctor thought for a moment. 'Can I see it?'

'How can you see it?'

'Will you trust me?'

Grace hesitated. Then she nodded again, subtly but surely.

The Doctor stepped forward and gently rested his hands on Grace's temples. 'Close your eyes.'

'What are you doing?' she asked, following his instruction.

'Trust me,' said the Doctor. 'Picture what you saw in the water. Hold it in your mind. Can you see it?'

Grace trembled. 'Yes.'

The Doctor shut his eyes too and Grace gasped.

'You are inside my mind! How are you doing this?'

Fear Death by Water

The Doctor could see flashes of Grace's childhood memories: *the eider ducks waddling around their cottage; the joy of dancing to the jigs her father played on his fiddle; the grief of the first Christmas without her brother Job; the pride the first time she rowed the coble on her own.*

'I need you to focus only on what you saw in the water, Grace,' explained the Doctor. 'Try to shut away any other memories.'

'How do I do that?'

'Concentrate hard. Imagine closing doors. You are in control of your thoughts; they are not in control of you.'

The mental information shifted. Grace's long-term memories disappeared behind imaginary closed doors and her most recent recollections came to the fore: *the panic of spotting the wreckage on Big Harcar Rock; the longing to help the survivors; the rush of launching the coble; the fear of drowning in the stormy sea.* Then the Doctor saw it too: *the fire-eyes in the waves.*

The Doctor pulled his hands away. 'Open your eyes, Grace.' He whipped out his sonic screwdriver, scanning Grace's eyes.

'What are you doing?' asked Grace, instinctively turning her face away.

'Scanning,' said the Doctor. 'Face me.'

'Why? What is that... device?'

The Doctor read the results on the sonic. 'You're carrying a psychic spoor. The same psychic spoor I picked up on the captain.'

'Psychic spoor?' said Grace. 'What is it?'

A creature that burns itself inside the mind of anyone who looks it in the eye, thought the Doctor. 'It seems whatever you saw left an imprint. Animals do it all the time; they leave a trace, like a scent, or footprint. But this has left an imprint in your subconscious.'

'How do I get rid of it?' Grace asked.

'I don't know. Yet.' The Doctor could see Grace was doing her utmost not to panic.

Say something reassuring.

'Grace, can you smell something?'

Grace sniffed. 'Yes.'

'I thought I could smell it earlier.' The Doctor sniffed furiously, trying to source the scent. 'It's been bugging me all day. It's sort of musky…'

'Like old, sweaty leather,' Grace added.

The Doctor wafted the aura into his nostrils. 'It's you, Grace.'

Grace leaned forward and smelt the Doctor. 'No, it's *you*.'

'It is not *me*!' the Doctor protested. 'I'm wearing Gallifreyan Goddess. Best perfume in the galaxy.' River Song had left a bottle in the TARDIS many years ago, and although the scent regenerated on a daily basis to suit the Doctor's mood, it always reminded him of her. Today it was a seductive mix of sea salt, vanilla and sandalwood, with a base note of oud and…

A sour-smelling musk.

'What?!' The Doctor screwed up his face in disgust, as he sniffed his arms. 'You're right.'

'You said animals leave a trace like a scent…'

The Doctor scanned the full length of Grace's body, up and down, frowning at the reading. Then he thrust the sonic screwdriver at Grace. 'Here. Press this button, and do what I did.'

'I cannot fathom what this device of yours is for.' Nevertheless, Grace copied the Doctor's motion, moving the sonic across his body.

'Let me see what it's saying.' The Doctor grabbed his sonic back and read the results. 'The spoor's on me too. How? I didn't see the creature. Well, I saw it in your mind, but that doesn't count.' He thought, tapping one finger against his lips. 'This spoor is different. It's an odorous residue. And it's on both of us. Which means we've both been near it.'

'Perhaps we acquired it in the same place,' said Grace.

'Which would mean…'

The Doctor turned and scampered down the stairs, Grace hurrying along behind as he bundled into the living area, immediately starting to scan the survivors. The smell of mothballed blankets and bergamot and potatoes was strong in the room, but behind it, that faint sour aroma she'd not noticed before.

'Everybody who was on the rock has been exposed,' said the Doctor.

Grace peeped into the kitchen and saw her mother

dozing in her chair at the table. Gently she took her mother's hand and inhaled. 'Nothing. Because Mam didn't go.'

'Yes, that must be it,' said the Doctor. 'That creature you saw – it left a trace of itself in the sea. And we've followed in its wake. What *was* that creature? How much did you see, Grace? What did it look like?'

'I only saw its eyes,' Grace replied.

Again, the Doctor thought back to the captain's words. *A beast is rising from the deep.* 'I need to get back to my ship…'

'Your ship? You were on the *Forfarshire*.'

'Ah. Long story.'

'Tell it. We've got all night.'

'We haven't,' said the Doctor, running back up the stairs to the lantern room, Grace hot on his tail. He swiped the barometer.

'Doctor, what on earth do you think you are doing? Put that back.'

'I need to go,' said the Doctor. 'My ship is on the rock. I need some mercury to repair the fluid link, which is why I need this barometer. I can get it back to you in five minutes. Probably. Give or take.'

'You can't get to the rock and back in five minutes,' said Grace.

'Just watch me. We need to track down this creature. See what it is we're dealing with.'

'Stop,' said Grace. 'Doctor, it's getting dark now, you

cannot go out there, not in this weather. I know I am linked to this creature in some way; if something happens to you, neither one of us will learn the truth. Please. I'll gladly aid you, but let's wait until the storm subsides.'

'I hate waiting,' said the Doctor, pouting as he looked down at the barometer.

'Then you must learn to be better at it.'

Maybe the universe is trying to teach me a lesson, the Doctor thought. He had been forced to wait a year at the Sandringham Hotel. To his great surprise, he had even quite enjoyed it. Surely he could manage to stay a few days at Longstone Lighthouse…

Chapter Eight
The Dead Sea

'What do you think?' said the Doctor, modelling his new hand-knitted scarf: a multicoloured array of purple, camel, mustard, rust, grey, greenish brown and bronze stripes.

It was the second evening at Longstone Lighthouse. The other survivors had retired to their beds of straw that the Darlings had made up in the old barracks next to the lighthouse. Meanwhile, the Doctor sat up with Mrs Darling, knitting.

'Surprisingly good!' said Mrs Darling, peering over her half-moon spectacles. 'For a gentleman.'

'I learnt from the best,' said the Doctor.

'Did your mother teach you?'

'My mother? No. Tom Daley. Gorgeous man.'

Mrs Darling peered at the empty sack beside him. 'You used all the wool?'

'You didn't tell me not to,' said the Doctor.

Mrs Darling laughed. 'Oh, you are a character, Doctor Smith. It's a lovely scarf. Just don't trip over it as you go.'

Go where? the Doctor thought. He had been stuck at Longstone Lighthouse for two days now, and he had cabin fever.

'Now, I must go to bed,' said Mrs Darling with a yawn. 'You should too, Doctor Smith. Go and get some rest.'

The trouble was, the Doctor didn't know how to rest. Knitting was a noble occupation, but he couldn't ignore his urge to investigate any longer.

'Help!'

The Doctor heard Grace's panicked cry from the kitchen and flew towards the commotion. She was lying on the kitchen table, flailing her arms around, as though struggling against an unseen threat. Her eyes were open, but she seemed to be still asleep.

'I can't breathe!' Grace gasped. 'I'm drowning!'

'You're not. You're having a night terror. Can you hear me, Grace?'

She didn't respond.

The Doctor scanned her as before. Whatever was residing in her subconscious, it was evolving, getting stronger. But why?

Abruptly, Grace sat bolt upright, panting. She opened her eyes. 'Doctor, I was sleeping, and a sudden heat fired through my mind.'

'The creature was in your mind again?'

'Yes, but the vision altered. For a moment, I was no longer seeing the eyes themselves, but I was seeing through the eyes.'

'And what did you see?'

'All I could see was dark water, deep in the ocean. And then I was drowning. The ocean began to consume me.'

Fear Death by Water

The Doctor recalled the captain's warning. *The ocean will consume us all.* 'We need to find out what it was you saw in the water,' he said.

'I don't know what it was,' said Grace. 'I told you.'

'My ship can identify it,' said the Doctor.

'How can a ship identify it?' asked Grace. 'A ship is not cognisant.'

'Mine is. Why are you sleeping on the kitchen table?' the Doctor asked, as Grace slid off it to go and make herself a camomile tea.

'Sarah Dawson and the children are still in my bed,' she replied. 'And I don't like to sleep on the floor. I'm afraid of flooding. Tea, Doctor?'

'No thanks.'

In the early hours of the following morning, the Doctor lay restlessly in his makeshift bed in the barracks. He unburied himself from the straw and snuck outside, grateful to be escaping all the snoring and snorting. Dawn was breaking.

The Doctor wrapped his new scarf around his neck, then manhandled the barometer into his coat pocket. He peered through the ground-floor window of the lighthouse, to check there was no one up and about who might thwart his escape plan. He could see only Grace, asleep on the kitchen table.

He felt bad for leaving without saying goodbye, and for going against his word. He had promised Grace he wouldn't wander off until after the storm was over. How many times had he given that instruction himself? Now he understood why his companions disobeyed him. It was a boring rule.

The Doctor headed for the boatshed, which was next to the barracks. He creaked the door open as quietly as he could. There was the Darlings' now-famous Northumberland coble.

Best not take that, the Doctor thought, knowing it needed to end up in the museum in one piece. He opted for the other old fishing boat inside.

He pulled it out from the boatshed and carried it overhead, towards the edge of the rock, then hopped in. The old boat bobbed in the water. The Doctor waited a moment to check its buoyancy before setting off. He knew someone would spot him from the lighthouse sooner or later, so he donned his intelligent gloves to ensure he could row as quickly as possible.

The Farne Islands were magnificent, in an oppressive sort of way, the Doctor thought as he rowed. He admired the uneven outcrops of black lava rock and the myriad birds that nested there. The islands had formed from magma that rose up through the cracks in the Earth's crust millions of years ago. *Wonder if I was there at the time...?*

He passed Clove Car first, then Little Harcar. Both rock tops were covered with guano, like liquid fondant icing drizzled on a dark chocolate cake, and there was an

Fear Death by Water

overpowering scent of uric acid and faeces mixed with salty sea air and there it was again... that sour-smelling musk. The odorous trail left by Grace's mysterious sea creature. *Where is it now?*

Doesn't the sea seem strange today? he wondered, as he rowed ever closer towards Big Harcar. The sea felt quiet. Almost empty. Like a watery wasteland. And then he realised he had entered the ships' graveyard. Lives had been lost here. Death affected a place.

All the dead bodies had disappeared. A chill passed through the Doctor's body. He thought of all the people he had failed to save on the *Forfarshire*. He thought again of James and Matilda. *Practise what you preach, Doctor*, he told himself, remembering how he had consoled Grace the other day.

Finally, there it was: the skeletal shipwrecked remains of the *Forfarshire*. The once-luxurious paddle steamer was now scarcely recognisable; its shattered hull a stark reminder of the unforgiving power of the sea.

A congregation of puffins, razorbills, guillemots, kittiwakes and terns soared overhead, squawking noisily as the Doctor pulled the trawler onto Big Harcar, then carefully clambered onto the wreckage of the *Forfarshire*'s bow, which was still breached on the rock. He made his way through tangled rigging across the lifeless timber frame until he reached his TARDIS.

The Doctor beamed at his indestructible ship. Then he noticed a grey tern perched territorially on top of the lantern, its black-tipped orange bill chipping away at the blue roof, which was splattered with white bird droppings.

'Get off!' shooed the Doctor. 'No more hitchhikers on the back of my TARDIS, thank you, please.' Then he entered his ship.

The door clicked shut behind him. The Doctor sniffed, assessing the faintly lingering scent of mercury fumes, but he was relieved to see that the failsafe had kicked in this time, and the interior hadn't shrunk to police-box size.

'Hey, honey. I'm home.' The Doctor grinned. He peeled off his burnt-orange leather trench coat, flinging it to one side, along with his new scarf, making a mental note to find a coat stand. *Yeah, right, that would happen!* He still hadn't got round to finding a chair. There were always far more important things to think about. *Feng shui* would have to wait.

The Doctor headed straight for the frazzled fluid link. He analysed the Darlings' barometer. A pool of toxic, silvery-white, dense metal liquid sat in a circular, shallow glass dish which surrounded a glass tube. The Doctor unsealed the top of the tube, and with great precision poured ten millilitres of mercury into the glass tube of the fluid link.

The TARDIS fired back to life. The Doctor smiled, relieved to see the central time rotor chugging up and down, as the spaceship dematerialised from the *Forfarshire*'s remains and touched down onto the solid surface of Big Harcar.

Fear Death by Water

He checked the console screen and frowned. There was something different about the rock. The fishing trawler had disappeared. He stepped outside, assessing that the weather had changed, too.

It was a brighter day. Sunny, even.

Coordinates must have shifted slightly when I materialised onto the rock, he thought. *How much time has passed?*

The Doctor nipped back inside and ran a scan of the waters surrounding the Farne Islands. After a few seconds, the scanner flashed and bleeped.

No sign of any unusual, extraterrestrial creatures. However…

'What?!' the Doctor exclaimed in disbelief.

According to the scanner fifty percent of ocean life within a 300-mile radius had disappeared. *That can't be.* The North Sea should be teeming with over 200 species of fish, marine mammals, crustaceans, phytoplankton and zooplankton, sea anemones and seahorses. It should be abundantly rich in its biodiversity. The Doctor ran the scan again, just to check that it wasn't a bogus result. But no. Half of the North Sea's creatures had vanished.

What if the beast has risen from the deep and consumed the ocean, and I've missed it?

The result from the scan also showed that the seawater was teeming with that same odorous spoor. *The creature's still knocking about here somewhere*, thought the Doctor. *But where – and what – is the source?*

Finding an unidentified creature in the North Sea was not going to be easy. Unless he was able to connect Grace to the TARDIS's telepathic circuits. Undoubtedly, she had a connection with this creature.

How far did it extend?

Chapter Nine
Feats of Female Fortitude

Grace stood by the wood stove in the kitchen watching the high-pressure steam erupt through the spout of the kettle. It had been three days since the Doctor had disappeared along with their barometer, and she was worried. He had been such a fool to take off like that.

She couldn't stop thinking about him. He had been inside her mind, after all. Then he'd told her about the psychic spoor within her, and what was she supposed to do about that? Just let it fester?

She was longing to speak with him, as she feared the mental intrusions were getting stronger.

They had sent out a search party, but the Doctor was nowhere to be found. Neither was that mysterious ship of his. The only vessels on the rock were the remains of the *Forfarshire* and, mysteriously, their old fishing boat, which they had since recovered. Grace knew that such strange goings-on must have *something* to do with him...

The other eleven *Forfarshire* survivors had left the lighthouse now too. They had been moved to the infirmary at Bamburgh Castle, and the Darlings' home was more or less their own again.

The kettle whistled, signalling it was time for tea.

'I'll serve,' said Mrs Darling, bustling over to the stove and ushering Grace towards the living area. 'You sit and talk to the men from the press. They're not interested in me. They're here to see you.'

Grace had hidden herself in the kitchen to avoid the three journalists sitting in the living area; leather-bound journals on their laps and leather briefcases by their sides. Now she took a stool beside her father as he spoke to the reporters. She stared absentmindedly into the teacup her mother handed her, blowing onto the hot liquid, watching as it rippled under the fan of her breath.

A nice cup of tea could usually calm her nerves. But not today. The men from the press made her feel uncomfortable. She'd never been interviewed before.

What will they ask me? What if I say the wrong thing? What if I clam up and say nothing at all?

A flash of the fire-eyes inflamed her anxious thoughts. *Ouch!* Grace burnt her mouth on the still-scalding tea.

'Grace Darling!' said one of the reporters, turning his questioning to her. 'The *Darling* of the Nation. That's good, write it down,' he added to one of his colleagues. 'What could be a more fitting name for a young heroine who possesses such fair beauty and a kind and courageous heart?'

'Oh,' Grace blushed and brushed off the praise. 'I assure you I am just an ordinary girl who helps my father look after the lighthouse.'

'And yet, your noble and heroic conduct saved lives.'

Grace smiled modestly but said nothing in reply. She fixated on a tiny crack in the china cup she was holding. The reporter pressed on:

'Describe to us the events of the morning of the 7th of September…'

Grace glanced over to her father, hoping he might speak for her, but all eyes were on her now, his included, waiting to hear her account.

'Well,' Grace started. Blood swelled in her freshly blistered bottom lip. 'I was the first to see the distressing affair. I immediately acquainted my father. We were most anxious. I rendered my father every assistance that lay in my power.'

'What was going through your mind at the time?'

'I believe I had very little thought of anything but to exert myself. My spirit was worked up by the sight of such a dreadful affair.'

'Your exertion was an extraordinarily impressive feat for a young woman,' declared the reporter. 'Wouldn't you agree?'

'I was simply doing my job,' Grace smiled. 'It's my duty. God's will. I can assure you, neither I nor my father need any recognition for our actions.'

'Well, well, well,' said Mr Darling, flicking through his copy of *The Times*, a week or so later. 'Listen to this: *It is impossible to speak in adequate terms of the unparalleled bravery and disinterestedness shown by Mr Darling and his truly heroic daughter, especially so with regard to the latter. Is there in the whole field of history, or of fiction, even one instance of female heroism to compare for one moment with this?'*

'Well, I never,' Mrs Darling beamed, as she sat at her spinning wheel, weaving. 'How about that then? Our Grace in the national newspaper!'

'She's in the local papers too,' said Mr Darling.

'What does it say?' Mrs Darling asked. 'Read it, William.'

'*As we approached the lighthouse, the heroine, Grace Darling herself, was descried high aloft, lighting the lamps, whose revolving illumination has warned so many an anxious mariner of the rocks and shoals around. We received a hearty welcome from old Mrs Darling—*'

'Old!' scoffed Mrs Darling. 'How rude!'

'*– and her dauntless daughter. But Grace is nothing masculine in her appearance, although she has so stout a heart. In person she is about the middle size, of a comely countenance – rather fair for an islander – and with an expression of benevolence and softness most truly feminine in every point of view. When we spoke of her noble and heroic conduct, she slightly blushed, and appeared anxious to avoid the notice to which it exposed her.*'

Grace blushed again with embarrassment. These words *did* expose her and she didn't like it one bit. What did they mean, she was 'nothing masculine in her appearance'?

What did that have to do with anything?

'This must be why so many people have been writing to you,' said Mr Darling. 'They must have read about you in the paper.'

'I wish they wouldn't,' Grace sighed, remembering the huge pile of letters on her desk that she still had to reply to. 'I don't like the idea of people knowing all about us.'

'I should imagine all the fuss will die down soon,' said Mr Darling, returning his attention to the paper.

'I hope so,' said Grace quietly.

'You should be extremely proud, Grace,' said Mrs Darling. 'We are.'

Grace retreated upstairs to her bedroom. She didn't want to hear anything else that was written about her in the newspapers today. All this attention from the press and the public since the rescue was starting to become a bit much.

How grateful she was for her remote hideaway. She sat at the mahogany desk in her bedroom, twirling her hair with her fingers as she gazed through her window.

The sight of the sea comforted her. It was calm today. Unusually so.

Grace pulled a strand of her long hair taut, picked up a pair of scissors and snipped off a small clump.

She held this piece of herself in the palm of her hand, looking at it for a moment, as though trying to decide what to do with it.

Then she carefully slipped the lock into an envelope, picked up a fountain pen, dipped it into the inkwell and began to write:

> *Dear Madam,*
>
> *I received your kind sum of ten pounds and beg to return my most sincere thanks and grateful acknowledgements. I felt very much for you when you mentioned the loss of your late friend who perished on the steamship* Forfarshire, *but we must put our trust in God.*
>
> *You requested that I let you know whether I felt pleasure to be out in a rough sea, which I can assure you there is none to any person in their sober senses. I have often had occasion to be in the boat with my Father for want of better help, but never at the saving of any lives before, and I pray to God may never be again.*
>
> *As requested, please accept a lock of my hair, as a small memorandum.*
>
> *Your ever Obliged Humble Servant,*
> *G. H. Darling*

Grace sealed the letter and placed it to one side.

The other side of the desk was buried under a large pile of post. These well-wishers had taken such trouble to write to her. She felt a lock of her hair was a reasonable token of thanks, in exchange for the generous gifts they were sending her. She was about to snip the next lock, when the burning sensation in her eyes flared up yet again.

Fear Death by Water

The daylight streaming in through the window suddenly felt blindingly bright. Grace closed her eyes. But in the darkness, there they were once again: the beastly fire-eyes.

'Go away!' she cried, holding her head in her hands. 'Stop! Please!'

Grace rigorously massaged her temples and took a few deep breaths to try to calm herself down. She decided she would write to her favourite sister, Thomasin, instead.

Dearest Sister,

I regret that it has been a while since I've written. I cannot keep up with my correspondence. Since the rescue, I have so many letters to respond to. People write most kindly, though in truth, I find the attention suffocating. However, if I do not respond, I fear that I am letting good people down.

As public interest increases, so do my anxieties. I know I can confide in you, dearest Thomasin: since the rescue, I have suffered from an affliction beyond my comprehension. The most terrifying vision – the blazing eyes of a beast in the ocean – is consuming my thoughts, my nightmares. At times, it is so intense that I...

She was halfway through her sentence when something on Big Harcar Rock caught her eye. She went over to the window, opened it and stuck out her head.

Next to the remains of the *Forfarshire*, what was that? She grabbed her telescope.

A strange blue box had appeared on the rock, seemingly out of nowhere. A man stepped out from it. She squinted through the glass. It was the Doctor! He stood on the rock next to the box, then after a few seconds, he disappeared back into it.

Chapter Ten
The Subconscious Monster

The Doctor rummaged around in the TARDIS's massive wardrobe for his brass and rubber diving suit. He brushed a few loose grey hairs from the helmet – remnants of a younger man – and clambered into the cumbersome outfit, which felt appropriate for the period as well as the occasion.

He threw open the TARDIS doors and stepped outside. Then he saw her.

Grace was standing on the rocks next to her coble and oars. She tightened the wrap of her shawl around her shoulders, looked at the blue box behind him and frowned. 'Where on earth have you been?'

'On this rock,' said the Doctor.

'For two weeks?'

He pulled a face. 'Time slipped by.'

'I said I'd aid you once the storm had subsided.'

'Well then, the sun's out, let's crack on.'

'What are you doing in this... this boatshed?'

'Boatshed? It looks nothing like a boatshed.'

Grace guessed again. 'A wardrobe?'

'No, but there is a wardrobe inside,' said the Doctor.

'First door on the left, second right, under the stairs, past the bins, fifth door on the left. Why would there be a wardrobe on a rock? This is my ship.'

'Doctor, I don't know if you are experiencing delusions, or suffering from exposure, but this box is not in any shape or form a ship.'

'I'll show you.' He pulled open the door and stepped inside. 'Come on in!' he called back to her.

Grace entered the box.

The Doctor looked at her expectantly. 'I love this part,' he said as Grace's jaw dropped open in awe. 'What do you think?'

'It's…' Grace didn't have the vocabulary to describe it. 'How is it so…'

'Impressive? Majestic? Awe-inspiring? Much bigger on the inside? It's called the TARDIS. Time And Relative Dimension in Space.'

Grace walked round the console, taking it in.

'You call yourself the Doctor,' said Grace. 'What are you a doctor of, exactly?'

'Everything. I'm a traveller.'

'But how can something like this move? I don't understand.'

'Grace, there are things in this universe I've been trying to understand for centuries, and trust me, you always end up with far more questions than answers. Want my advice? Embrace everything with an open mind, especially the things you don't understand.'

Grace still wasn't quite satisfied. 'If this is a ship then how does it sail?'

'It sails through space. Kind of. Among other things. It can take me to any rock in the universe.'

'And you chose to come to this one?'

'Well, no. Actually, I was aiming for Longstone. But the storm threw me off course and I landed up on the *Forfarshire*.'

'Why did you want to come to Longstone? There's nothing there.'

'There's something to find wherever you go, if you look for it. There's so much life beyond these shores. Though around these shores, right now, there's not as much as there should be.'

'What do you mean?'

'I reckon that sea creature of yours has had a big lunch. How is the…?' The Doctor tapped his temple.

Grace hesitated. 'I fear it is getting worse. What is happening to me?'

'I'm going to find out,' said the Doctor. 'With your cooperation and some help from my ship.'

Grace looked at the Doctor with mild scepticism.

'You can trust me,' he assured her.

Eventually Grace nodded. 'I want to help. What do you need me to do?'

The Doctor smiled. 'Have you heard of mesmerism?'

'The theory that all living things have an animal magnetism – an invisible, natural force.'

'Bang on!' the Doctor declared. 'Named for Franz Mesmer. Lovely guy. Threw the best picnics. And what I have in mind for your mind is a bit like that. Not the picnic part,' he added. 'The invisible, natural force that can be harnessed... and used for healing.'

'Your own natural force?'

'My TARDIS is much more than just a ship, remember? You'll see.' He pressed a green button on the console. 'Initiating telepathic circuits... Grace, I need you to put your hands just here, on the console. Don't worry, it won't hurt.'

Grace carefully placed her hands where the Doctor had pointed. She pressed and held down the two blue buttons, which sat either side of the green.

'There's a strange tingling in the back of my head,' said Grace.

'Just the telepathic interface saying hello. You're forming a link with my ship.' The Doctor pressed the yellow button on the far right of the panel. 'Activating telepathic circuits...'

'What do I need to do?' Grace asked.

'Nothing – your subconscious and the TARDIS telepathic circuits are already doing it. The vision may appear intensely in your mind.'

Grace screwed her eyes tightly shut. 'I can see... something...'

'Try to hold on to whatever it is,' said the Doctor. 'Oh, yes! Grace, it's working!'

Fear Death by Water

Grace could hear the Doctor speaking as if from far away. Her mind felt like it was emptying, cogent thought washed away by saltwater cold as ice.

All she knew was hunger, power and speed.

She gasped, gulping down the ocean. Prey was close by and she turned, propelled herself towards it. A whole shoal couldn't fill her throat and while she gloried in the taste of raw flesh she needed more, *more*...

The darkness of the deep sea filled her to the brim. Grace collapsed.

When her eyes opened again, Grace saw all the impossible marvels of the Doctor's fantastical home. She breathed air that smelled of scent, not of the sea. The phantasmagoria she'd witnessed was fading like a dream, but inside her soul Grace felt bruised black and blue.

'What happened,' she breathed. 'I was... Doctor, what was I...?'

'Easy, easy now.' The Doctor was beside her in a flash, looking into her eyes. 'You did so well. Grace Darling, a-maze-*ing*!' He laughed as he jumped up and hit the controls. 'The TARDIS got enough from you to dig up some deets on the species. Look!'

Grace looked up groggily at the screen that the Doctor was pointing to. It showed the image of a shadowy, serpentine form with fiery eyes. Beside it, strange symbols were resolving themselves into words she found she could understand.

'The Leviathan?' Grace breathed. 'I know that name from Father's Bible lessons when we were children. A sea serpent…'

'The mother of *all* sea serpents,' said the Doctor. 'The Leviathan appears in all sorts of ancient texts and mythologies. One of three primordial forces spawned from the chaotic essence of the beginning of things. There's Behemoth, the Beast of the Earth. Ziz, the Beast of the Air. And Leviathan, the Beast of the Sea.'

'But that's just a story.'

'There's always some truth to stories. They're how early civilisations tried to understand the natural world. The ocean was vast and mysterious. Dangerous. Impossible to control. The Leviathan is the manifestation of all the fears of the sea wrapped into one entity. An embodiment of chaos.'

'But where did it come from?' asked Grace.

The Doctor glanced back at the screen, which was now swimming with data.

'Point of origin is unknown,' he muttered. 'Oh, but it's old. As old as the oldest oceans in the universe…'

'That ancient serpent, who is called the Devil and Satan,' said Grace, uneasily recalling a verse from the Book of Revelation. 'Whatever it is, Doctor, where's it been all this time?'

'Who knows,' said the Doctor. 'Dormant. Hiding. There are thousands of water worlds in your galaxy alone…'

He tailed off, frowning, as an unearthly caterwauling began to rend the air about them.

Grace's hands flew to her ears. 'What's that noise?'

'The TARDIS is dematerialising,' said the Doctor, running round the console. 'I didn't set the controls. I can't stop it. Something is taking us away!'

Chapter Eleven
The Twilight Zone

The Doctor cautiously creaked open the door to his ship and peeked round.

'Okay,' he said, pulling back the door. 'Grace, you know I was talking about all the life on different shores? Well, you're about to see some of it.'

'Out there on Big Harcar Rock?'

'That's the thing. We're not on the rock any more.'

'We're not?'

'My ship moves from one place and reappears in another. We've moved. Just now.'

'But that's impossible.'

'Brilliant, you mean. Look!'

Grace peered through the crack. They were in some sort of narrow passageway. Wonky copper pipes interwoven with organic coral tendrils snaked along the ceiling and translucent walls, which glistened and pulsed faintly as though they were alive, imbuing the space with a golden and green glow. It looked alien. Magical.

'Where are we?' Grace asked, feeling a mix of both excitement and trepidation.

'Someone else's ship,' said the Doctor.

'Whose?'

'I don't know.' The Doctor grinned, stepping out. 'Wanna find out?'

Grace hesitated.

The Doctor looked back at her expectantly. 'Open that mind, Grace!' he said. 'And shut the door behind you!'

Grace's initial twinge of excitement quickly dissipated as she followed the Doctor through the passageway. She felt a wave of giddy claustrophobia. Like she was trapped in a nightmare. She rubbed her temples. She could sense the fire eyes flaring again. *This can't be real*, she thought to herself. This must all be a bad dream. She blinked rapidly, trying to jolt herself awake, back to reality.

When the Doctor turned to Grace, she could see the warmth and kindness in his eyes, and it made her feel a little reassured.

'Hey. It's all right,' he told her. 'I know this is a big adjustment.'

'Adjustment? It's beyond belief!'

'That's what makes it fun,' the Doctor countered. 'You'll have a million questions. But if you ask them all now, you'll miss the moment.'

Grace tensed. 'Doctor,' she whispered. She could hear the padding of steps approaching from behind them.

The Doctor spun on his heels. 'Oh, hello!'

Grace glanced over her shoulder then slowly turned round. Her senses tried to shy from what she saw, rooted her to the spot.

Standing before them was a tall, slender creature that might have stepped from the pages of a child's storybook. He certainly didn't look like any man she had ever seen before. He had bioluminescent scaly cerulean skin, a long, thin face with wide emerald eyes and clear eyelids, and lithe webbed limbs. He wore a tunic that looked like it was made from scraps of seaweed, and a badge displaying the emblem of a compass marked with peculiar glyphs.

'Nice ship you've got here!' said the Doctor, keeping the tone light. 'Very Captain Nemo.'

'Nemo is not the captain of this ship,' said the tall man. He exuded an ethereal air of elegance and authority.

'No, I'm assuming that would be you,' said the Doctor.

'I am Ketor of ISC Division Kappa.' The emblem on his chest glowed gold.

'I'm the Doctor, citizen of the universe, and a hell of a guy to boot. And this is my new friend, Grace Darling of Longstone Lighthouse.'

'Hello,' Grace said nervously.

'And who's that?' asked the Doctor. Another slender man was scanning the Doctor's blue box, which was parked at the far end of the passageway.

'That is Chip, also of Division Kappa. Stay here.'

'Doctor,' Grace whispered, as Ketor strode off to join his associate. 'They look exactly the same but they... they can't be human?'

'Course not. They're Thalassians,' said the Doctor.

'But they...'

'They come from a water world a hundred lightyears from Earth, called Thalassa. Also known as TOI-1452b. It orbits one of two small stars in a binary system located in the Draco constellation. Gorgeous planet, Thalassa. I've always wanted to visit. They have the calmest oceans in the universe.'

'What's the ISC?' Grace asked.

'Intergalactic Sea Corps.'

'A military unit?'

'Yep. Authorised by the Shadow Proclamation to protect the galaxy's oceans from extraterrestrial threats and terrors.'

'And what's the Shadow Proclamation?'

'A million questions!'

The Thalassians came back over.

'We took this to be a life-pod of some kind,' said Chip, excitement in his eyes; his general demeanour was less forbidding than Captain Ketor's. 'But it's reading as a craft bigger inside than out.'

The Doctor winked at Grace. 'Some people just get it.' Then he smiled a little self-consciously and took a step closer to the Thalassians. 'Why hijack my ship?'

A loud beeping echoed from another room.

'We must attend,' said Ketor. 'Follow.'

With a shrug of his shoulders, the Doctor did just that. Grace went with him, trailing the Thalassians through various compartments of the seaship.

'Doctor, have we been kidnapped?' Grace whispered.

'Kidnapped, or pressganged,' said the Doctor.

Soon, he and Grace found themselves crammed into the confined, dimly lit control room of the Thalassian seaship. Ketor and Chip had already taken their positions in the two high-backed pilots' chairs, adorned with intricate gears and twining tendrils. They sat in front of the wide brass console which boasted an array of cogs, levers, dials and touch pads, and displayed glowing glass interfaces, navigation charts and display screens.

'*Buoyoncé*: incoming report from Judoon vessel on Marinus,' announced a female voice.

Ketor tapped one of the screens and the beeping stopped.

Grace jumped. 'Who said that?'

'*Buoyoncé*?' the Doctor grinned, crossing over to the bridge. 'Seriously?'

'It's the name of our ship,' said Chip with a small, knowing smile.

'Probably the best name for a ship, ever!' enthused the Doctor. 'I didn't know Queen B was a star in the Draco constellation...'

'Everywhere!' said Chip. Ketor rolled his eyes.

Grace frowned. 'But Victoria is queen...'

The Doctor laughed. 'Not got quite the same moves.'

'But—?'

'A million questions.' The Doctor pressed a finger to his lips and smiled. 'One moment. Circling back to the Judoon...'

'They've reported a possible sighting of the Leviathan on Marinus,' said Ketor, reading the alien glyphs on the display screen.

'The Leviathan?' said Grace.

'The Shadow Proclamation has deployed units to water worlds across the galaxy to track it down,' explained Ketor. 'We were assigned to Earth.'

'You're not so far away from home after all, Grace,' said the Doctor, studying the navigation chart. 'Relatively speaking. We're still in the North Sea at least.'

'The Leviathan is flitting between the seas of the cosmos,' said Chip. 'It must be contained before it wipes out any more ocean planets.'

'More?' said the Doctor.

'The Leviathan destroyed Thalassa,' said Chip quietly.

'What?' said the Doctor, scrolling through the ISC reports.

'What happened?' asked Grace.

'The population of Thalassa was decimated,' said Ketor. 'Drowned. Consumed by the Leviathan.'

'I had no idea,' said the Doctor. 'I'm so sorry. How many died?'

'Millions.' Ketor shook his head. 'After the bloodshed, any Thalassians who survived the slaughter soon began to starve. The Leviathan had consumed all our supplies. We lost everything. Chip, my brother, is all I've got left.'

'Once it got bored of killing us,' Chip continued, 'it vanished from our ocean and obliterated our sister planet.'

'Enaiposha too?' said the Doctor.

'Every Enaiposhian ocean boiled away to plasma,' said Chip. 'We qualified with the ISC during the rescue operations. Saw the horror first-hand.'

The Doctor recognised the pain on the Thalassian's face. 'We'll help you if we can,' he said. 'You didn't have to drag us here. So why did you?'

'We were scanning for traces of the Leviathan,' said Ketor. 'It doesn't register as a corporeal entity, though. Our tech cannot "see" the creature. It can only be seen in the flesh.'

That's why it didn't show up when I scanned the ocean, thought the Doctor. 'It's a sea creature from way, way back. Bound to have picked up some tricks.'

'Eventually, we picked up a trace,' said Chip. 'A kind of telepathic signal.'

'Ah,' said the Doctor. 'That would be Grace, connected to my ship. What you picked up on is some sort of a psychic link between her and the Leviathan.'

'And the beast itself eludes us still,' Ketor muttered.

'I saw the Leviathan, you see,' said Grace. 'In the flesh. Only once. Only briefly.'

'Where?' asked Chip.

'It was just off Big Harcar Rock,' she replied. 'But that was weeks ago.'

'If your link to the Leviathan is strong enough for our systems to track in on you,' said Ketor, 'perhaps together we can find this beast and deal with it once and for all.'

Grace felt a cold, webbed hand on her shoulder, as Ketor guided her into his pilot's seat. 'Sit,' he said. 'It connects the pilot directly to *Buoyoncé*'s systems.'

Chip pressed a button, and the canopy that was covering the domed observation deck rose, revealing a panoramic view of an underwater expanse. Grace pulled her attention to the complex instrumentation on the console in front of her.

'I can't pilot your ship!' she exclaimed.

'You do not need to do anything,' said Ketor.

'Intuitive control,' said Chip.

'Like my telepathic circuits,' said the Doctor. 'Just sit back, relax, and— *whoooooooaaaa!*'

All of a sudden, the seaship charged forward, like a bullet out of a gun. The momentum was visceral. Thrilling and terrifying. It was faster than Grace had ever travelled before. Her mother's potato soup from earlier churned in her stomach and the inside of her mind rushed – a wild blur of sea and the Leviathan's fire – as the seaship jerked and swerved, zigzagging through the water. Grace clasped hold of the arms of the chair.

Finally, the ship pulled to a halt, throwing Grace's head backwards.

'So much for sit back and relax,' said the Doctor. 'Everyone okay?'

'We've never connected an earthling to the system before,' said Chip.

'That's probably why,' said Ketor.

'You okay, Grace?' asked the Doctor.

Grace stood up from the pilot's seat. 'I'm all right. A little dizzy, that's all.'

'Here,' said Chip, handing her a small container. 'Drink this. It will help.'

Grace sipped the thick green liquid through a metal straw. It tasted like peaches and seaweed. She couldn't tell if she liked it or not, but she felt a restoring energy bubble through her. As she sipped again, she gazed through the observation window at the deep, dark sea.

She shuddered.

It was like being in another world. A liminal place of transition, longing, danger, the unknown. All those ancient civilisations that feared and wondered what might lurk beneath the surface. Now here she was eons later, staring into the watery abyss, still wondering herself.

'There's nothing out there,' she whispered, as though the Leviathan might hear her and jump out at them at any moment.

A deafening roar echoed like a tempest under the sea. The ominous low vibration sent shivers through the body of the seaship, and its passengers. It made every hair on Grace's body stand up on its end.

'You were saying?' said the Doctor.

Chapter Twelve
Force of Nature

'I am the ocean,' said the Doctor, frowning in deep concentration.

'What?' asked Ketor.

'Not me,' said the Doctor. 'The Leviathan.'

'How can you possibly know that?' asked Chip.

'Skills.' The Doctor shrugged. 'I speak whale; the dialect's similar.'

'But it's just noise,' said Grace.

'Everything's just noise unless you know how to listen.' The Doctor crouched down and placed his ear to the floor of the observation deck as the roar rumbled on. 'No, wait. It's saying: I *have* the ocean. I have the ocean's soul.'

Abruptly, a seismic shockwave rippled through the ocean and the sea began to churn. The Doctor sprang back up to his feet and pressed his face against the viewport. A vortex was forming ahead. But it was more than just a natural eddy. It was monstrously fast already. And it was growing stronger.

Remaining calm and composed, Ketor and Chip jumped to attention, resuming their positions in the pilots' seats.

'Turn the ship around right now!' shouted the Doctor. 'Direct the full engine power away from the outer edge.'

But the force of the whirlpool was inescapable. The water frothed and twisted as though it were alive, gripping the *Buoyoncé* and dragging it nose first into a massive spiral of swirling water.

At the deep heart of the vortex, a shadow emerged.

'The Leviathan!' cried Grace.

The Doctor could see it, emerging from the abyss, coiling through the dark water like a living nightmare made flesh, its eyes piercing through the storm it had summoned.

'*Buoyoncé*, ISC Division Kappa reporting confirmed sighting of the Leviathan on Earth,' said Ketor, tapping details into one of the organic touch screens on the control deck. 'Sending coordinates now.'

'Tell them to send backup,' said the Doctor.

Chip shook his head. 'Galactic comms are down.'

'The system is too strained,' said Ketor. '*Buoyoncé*'s in failsafe mode.'

A metallic groan creaked through the hull as the water pressure outside mounted and the sea started spiralling with frightening velocity.

'You need to go against the flow,' said Grace.

'Use the thrusters,' the Doctor shouted. 'You've got to steer perpendicular to the whirlpool's rotation and escape the spiral trajectory.'

'We're trying!' said Ketor. 'The thrusters are damaged.'

'And the engine's drained, we need more power,' Chip added. 'I told you we shouldn't have—'
Chip shot his brother a look and cleared his throat.
'Shouldn't have what?' said the Doctor.
'Nothing. I'll go to the engine room, see if there's anything we can do to boost it manually,' said Chip.
'No, I'll go,' said Ketor. 'It's my responsibility.'
'Whatever you're doing, do it quickly,' cried Grace.

From the observation deck, Grace watched in horror as the Leviathan coiled itself around the seaship. The sea stopped spinning and, now it had them in its grasp, Grace saw the beast in its full glory.
It was colossal. A gargantuan serpentine body covered in thick impenetrable scales that shimmered like liquid metal. The Leviathan reared its huge black head and flicked its tail, which was armed with towering sharp spikes. It snaked around and looked at its prey with its searing orbs, emitting an eerie otherworldly light into the dim expanse.
'Don't look at its eyes,' Chip warned.
'It's the teeth I'm looking at!' said the Doctor.
Two rows of jagged yellow fangs filled its cavernous maw, a writhing, monstrous tongue and, past that, the dark hole of the Leviathan's gullet. Releasing the seaship from the hold of its tail, the Leviathan surged forwards, about to snap its jaw shut.
Grace screamed and jumped behind the Doctor, who in turn jumped into Ketor's pilot seat.

'Sharp starboard!' he yelled to Chip. With some nifty intuitive manoeuvring and just enough thrust, they swerved the seaship out of the way, in the nick of time.

'Sorry, Levi,' said the Doctor, 'we're not on the menu today.'

'The thrusters did not like that,' said Chip.

'Neither did the Leviathan,' said Grace.

The Leviathan roared in frustration and the force of the sound waves propelled the seaship backwards through the water.

'We need to contain it,' said the Doctor.

'I rather think it's containing us,' said Grace, watching as the Leviathan circled the seaship.

'It's toying with us,' said Chip.

'How can we contain it?' wondered the Doctor aloud. 'I'm thinking, some sort of sonic cage. Is that possible? Chip, what have you got on this ship?'

'Well... I've actually been thinking about how to contain the Leviathan for a while now, experimenting, and I've been developing some new tech.'

'Talk to me!' said the Doctor.

'Sonic drones,' Chip continued, 'containing a near infinite length of Enaiposhian cable.'

'Love it!' said the Doctor. 'Keep talking.'

'It's virtual, and harmless – unlike some sonar – but powerful.'

'Powerful enough to hold a force of nature?' asked the Doctor.

'That's the plan,' said Chip, 'but the tech has not yet been tested.'

'Then let's test it,' the Doctor replied. 'Use the drones to encircle the Leviathan and create our own cage. Grace, keep an eye on Levi for us. Chip, prepare those drones.'

'On it,' said Chip. 'Ordinarily, the drones are autonomous, they can operate without anyone in the loop.'

'But the Leviathan doesn't register on any systems,' said the Doctor, 'so I'm assuming we can operate them manually from here?'

'Precisely!' said Chip, detaching two handsets from the console. 'They're remote control. Fully charged, so they won't rely on power from the ship.'

'Excellent!' said the Doctor, taking a handset. He pressed a button and a drone released from the back of the seaship, swiftly followed by another operated by Chip.

The drones zoomed through the water. Two sleek, black bubbles. The Leviathan darted after them. Then it got bored of chasing the drones, and it went for the seaship.

Grace jumped into a pilot's seat and steered as far away from the Leviathan as she could. But the ship kept veering off course.

'How's the steering got worse?' asked the Doctor, taking the seat next to her to help navigate.

'The thrusters are completely trashed,' said Chip.

The Leviathan whipped its tail, repeatedly thrashing the seaship with the supernatural strength of its spikes. Batting it back and forth, flicking it up and down. A spike crushed into the outer hull.

A red warning light flashed on the control panel.

'Water intrusion detected in the engine room,' said Chip. 'Tor!'

He thrust his handset to Grace and swept out of the room.

'Ketor!' said Chip, bursting into the engine room.

'The seal's compromised,' Ketor reported.

The whole hull juddered as the Leviathan whacked the *Buoyoncé* again with its spiky tail, compromising the seal further.

'We need to get out of here,' said Chip, looking anxiously at the seawater that was already beginning to gush in through the torn seal.

'I need to repair the engine,' said Ketor, still assessing the damage.

'You should have thought about that earlier,' said Chip. 'Tor, I told you that blast would drain us. I knew it would be dangerous.'

'So let me fix it,' said Ketor.

Chip could see his brother was hellbent. No doubt he felt this was his responsibility, his penance. Chip could feel the water level rising around his lower legs. It was warm and stank of the Leviathan's spoor.

Fear Death by Water

Another heavy impact as the Leviathan came in hard. Seawater cascaded over the machinery as another seal burst, creating dangerous sparks and short circuits, and filling the room with the bitter smell of burning wires and smoke mixed with the briny scent of seawater. The engine sputtered. Its hum extinguished by a deafening rush of water.

The engine room plunged into complete darkness.

With a final swoop, the Leviathan smashed its tail into the *Buoyoncé*. The propellers stopped spinning and the seaship lost its propulsion. But it didn't sink. It was held in stasis, impaled on the Leviathan's tail.

The Leviathan roared, its eyes blazing.

Then suddenly, it stopped still. It blinked and simply stared at the seaship.

Grace trembled, realising that the creature wasn't just staring at the ship; it was staring at *her*.

Grace stared back through the observation window.

It was like she was in some sort of trance with the Leviathan. Initially, she felt that familiar burning sensation behind her eyes. But as their locked gaze intensified, the burn dissipated and it felt like the sea was rushing through her, a power that was somehow both chaotic and calm all at once. She felt like she was inside the Leviathan's mind.

Because for a long, intense moment, it felt like they were connected. Two spirits of the sea.

* * *

In the pitch black of the engine room, Ketor could hear his brother crying in pain. He waded through the gushing water, fumbling in the dark. 'Chip! Where are you? What's happened?'

'Gah!' Chip yelled, agonised.

'Chip!' said Ketor, stumbling over his brother's legs. 'What is it?' Under the rising water, he ran his hands along Chip's body, feeling for an injury. He stopped dead when he felt the end of a sharp spike protruding through Chip's abdomen.

The Leviathan hadn't just impaled his ship; it had impaled his brother.

'Pull me off this thing,' said Chip breathlessly. 'Do it. Quickly.'

Desperately, Ketor obeyed. Chip let out a blood-curdling cry as his brother eased him off the Leviathan's deadly spike. Then, Chip slumped, splashing into the rising water.

Ketor helped him to his feet, put his arm around him and the pair staggered towards the bulkhead. The water level was nearly up to their waists now, rapidly flooding and spilling into the adjacent compartments.

'We need to seal this bulkhead,' Chip panted, as they reached the door. 'Stop the entire vessel from flooding. Get back to the control room. Find the Doctor. Use the drones.'

'The system's malfunctioning,' Ketor retorted. 'We can only seal the bulkhead from the inside. We'll be trapped.'

Fear Death by Water

'We?' said Chip. And he shoved his brother across the threshold.

Ketor stumbled through into the adjacent compartment. But before he could even cry out to his brother, it was too late.

With all the final strength he could muster, Chip sealed the watertight door then collapsed into the flood.

Ketor hammered on the door. But he knew in his gut that his brother could no longer hear him. He pressed his face up to the tiny porthole. His heart sank. In the pitch blackness, he could just discern the pearlescent gleam of Chip's sightless eyes.

Chapter Thirteen
Blast to Kingdom Come

She isn't even blinking, thought the Doctor. He watched Grace carefully as she stared, entranced, at the Leviathan.

Are they communicating?

Some sort of psychic synchronisation?

Whatever it was, it was the perfect opportunity to create the sonic cage, so he took it.

The Doctor pulled Chip's remote control from Grace's fingers. Holding one handset in each hand, he frantically, but efficiently, navigated both drones. They zipped around the Leviathan in fast circles, encircling it in virtual cable.

'Activating sonic cage!' the Doctor announced, because it sounded cool. The virtual cable sparked to life.

Chip should be here to see this, the Doctor thought. He laughed, put down the controls and clapped his hands together. 'Yes! It's working!'

Grace snapped out of her trance with a groan and held her head in her hands.

'Hey! Are you okay?' the Doctor asked, coming to her side. 'Well done, you held the Leviathan while I cooked up the cage. What happened?'

'We were connected,' said Grace, her face haunted. 'It was terrifying at first. Those eyes burning into me. But I couldn't look away. I didn't want to look away. Neither did the Leviathan. It was as though it recognised me. Then it felt like I was no longer in the ocean. The ocean was in me... and I was in the Leviathan.'

Suddenly, the seaship shook violently. Now that the spell – or whatever it was with Grace – was broken, the Leviathan thrashed around inside its containment – with the seaship still attached to its tail. Grace tumbled to the floor. The Doctor steadied himself and flailed at the console, which was flashing chaotic signals.

'Doctor!' Grace cried.

Outside, the Leviathan's jaw was opening wide, baring its double row of jagged teeth.

'Can you do it again?' said the Doctor. 'Whatever it was you did just now? The allure, Grace! You can entrance it, calm it...'

'I don't know if I can,' said Grace.

Before she even had a chance to try, the Leviathan turned, bore down on the vessel impaled on its tail. With those terrifying teeth it plucked its prey free, and its jaws scissored down on the seaship.

'*Buoyoncé* systems critical,' came the calm computer voice. Danger lights flashed all around the control room as the water inside the Leviathan's maw dragged the seaship towards the back of the Leviathan's throat, a pulsing furnace of flesh.

Fear Death by Water

'We're getting outta here, Grace,' said the Doctor, grabbing the remote controls for the drones and sonic cage. 'Follow me, quickly!'

He flew out of the control room, and Grace staggered after him.

The whole seaship tilted as it slithered down the Leviathan's throat, groaning under the shifting pressure. Inside, clinging together, the Doctor and Grace slid down the sloping passageway, and crashed against the bulkhead that was sealing off the engine room.

The Doctor jumped to his feet, splashing in ankle-deep water. Shining his sonic through the porthole window, he peered into the engine room. 'It's completely flooded,' he reported.

'Are Ketor and Chip still inside?' said Grace, banging on the door.

'Hello?' yelled the Doctor. 'Chip! Ketor!'

Nothing. Except a gentle bouncing thud as the seaship landed on the soft, fleshy insides of the Leviathan's belly. They could no longer hear the sound of the sea, only an acidic fizz of enzymes as they got to work on digesting the hull.

'*Buoyoncé* systems critical,' the computer announced once more. Then something new: 'Warning. Sonar dome is engaged.'

'Sonar dome!' said the Doctor. 'We know where we are. What the hell are they doing in there?'

He darted off again.

Grace ran behind the Doctor, panting, struggling to keep up with his stride. She had never run so fast in her life. Her heart and head were pounding.

I'm inside an alien ship that's inside an alien beast!

The walls of the seaship were no longer glistening like they had been before; they were flashing red, alarms blaring. The Doctor and Grace ran along the passageway, down the stairs and into the sonar room in the lower front section of the ship.

It was like a smaller version of the bridge, studded with levers, switches and glass squares that danced with glowing text and images. Ketor was pressing his fingers to one of the screens, enlarging some shapes and shrinking others. A translucent dome rose from the control area. It encompassed a kind of sleek brass cannon which extended through the wall to project out into the darkness beyond.

'The sonar dome fires soundwaves out into the sea,' the Doctor told Grace. 'From the reflections, the ship can navigate the environment. But at full power those soundwaves work as a weapon. Soooo…'

He switched on his sonic screwdriver.

'Sonar dome disengaged,' announced *Buoyoncé*.

Ketor turned and frowned to see the Doctor and Grace standing in the entryway.

'Hi.' The Doctor waved his fingers. 'In case you missed it, we're inside the Leviathan's gut and the ship's systems are critical. You don't need a sonar sweep just now.'

'Ketor, where's Chip?' asked Grace.

'Dead,' snapped Ketor. 'He sealed himself in the engine room to prevent the whole ship flooding.'

Grace covered her mouth with her hands. 'Lord have mercy on his soul. He sacrificed himself?' She felt an overflow of gratitude – and guilt – that she was still alive, while Chip had perished.

If I'd calmed the Leviathan sooner, she thought, *would I have been able to save him from his fate?*

'Ketor, I'm sorry about your brother,' said the Doctor. 'But we need to go.'

'Chip is dead,' said Ketor, his voice heavy with grief.

'I know, and I'm so sorry. But revenge isn't the answer. If you're thinking of blasting the Leviathan from the inside with the sonar dome—'

'You've seen what it does for yourselves now!' Ketor shouted. 'The Leviathan will go on destroying, consuming, *desecrating*. The universe would be better off without it.'

'You don't get to decide that,' the Doctor said. 'This Leviathan is a complex creature. One of a kind. Or worse, the last of its kind.'

'I don't care,' Ketor spat.

'I think you do,' said Grace. 'I can see it in your eyes. You care about life.'

'It's why you do your job,' added the Doctor. 'It's why you took that ISC oath. But you can't be selective about which lives you care about, Ketor. That's not how it works.'

'Ketor, all lives are messy and chaotic in their own way,' said Grace. 'Yours, mine, the Leviathan's. That's what life is. Beauty and pain, we must embrace it all.'

Ketor turned away and jabbed again at the monitor.

'Sonar dome is engaged.'

'Ketor, that sonar dome emits soundwaves of over 500 decibels,' the Doctor said. 'It can rupture living matter!'

'That is the point.'

'What if the soundwaves get past the Leviathan? Earth is a classified Level 5 planet. Life in that ocean is precious. Marine life is already badly depleted because the Leviathan...'

Ketor looked away awkwardly.

'No.' The Doctor's voice hardened. 'It wasn't the Leviathan, was it? It was you! You've blasted this ocean before. That's what drained your ship's power.'

Ketor went on staring into the monitor.

'Ketor, honey, I'd love you to tell me I'm wrong right now.'

'I told you. We just couldn't locate the Leviathan.' Ketor hung his head. 'I had to attack from a wide range. It was the only option.'

'ISC laws forbid mass destruction of marine stocks on any world, let alone one not under your jurisdiction,' said the Doctor. 'You've messed up once, and now you're going to go again? Come on! We've contained it – the drones, the sonic cage, they worked! We just have to evacuate now and—'

'Fine.' Ketor reached back and tapped the screen. 'Evacuate.'

'Sonar dome is activated,' said *Buoyoncé*, her voice strained, wavering in pitch. 'Sonar strength maximum.'

'No!' The Doctor lunged for Ketor, who jumped up to block him. They tussled for a few seconds, until a severe metallic ping blasted out from the transducer in the sonar dome.

The Doctor let go of Ketor. There was a moment of stillness. Grace watched as his face fell. Sad, sullen.

'It's done,' Ketor said quietly.

Then the seaship bucked violently. Grace screamed as the most terrible pain shredded through her senses. She was ablaze but so cold. Sinking. Trapped and dying.

Blackness.

She came to on the floor. At first she thought herself paralysed. Everything was numb. But then an angry fizz of pins and needles made her writhe in agony. Above her, the ceiling began to buckle.

Then the Doctor was crouched over her, eyes full of concern. Not for himself. For her. He held her arms, whispered soothingly. 'You're here. You're all right.'

'Doctor, the Leviathan,' Grace whispered. 'It's fading from my mind.'

The ship lurched. Sparks exploded from the controls and a huge crack split the sonar dome.

'We need to get out,' the Doctor yelled. 'Now!'

Chapter Fourteen
Circle of Life

Grace clung to Ketor as he and the Doctor staggered through the disintegrating ship. The groaning of the hull sounded like a beast in terrible pain.

But that's outside *this vessel*, she thought.

'In, in, in,' said the Doctor, ushering them into his blue box.

Grace breathed a sigh of relief. Something about this bright, enormous room made her feel safe – as if anything were possible, even surviving so strange a predicament. Ketor walked around the console, taking it all in even as he held apart from Grace and the Doctor.

'Don't touch anything!' the Doctor warned them both. He checked certain instruments, then worked some of the controls.

Grace heard the same grating mechanical wheeze she had heard before. 'You're moving us to safety?'

But the Doctor was too focused to answer. The next moment, he ran to the door, pushed it open and leaned out into the open water.

'Goodness!' said Grace, following him over. She was amazed to see that they were still deep under the ocean, floating next to the Leviathan. The water was right outside the door, but it wasn't coming in. 'How?'

'I've extended the TARDIS's atmosphere,' the Doctor explained. 'It's like we're in a bubble.'

Through this bubble, they watched the Leviathan as it coiled itself into a tight, perfect circle. Grace frowned, confused, as its sharp fangs gently collapsed around the tip of its own tail. It seemed somehow both destructive and nurturing at the same time.

The Leviathan blinked slowly, once, then twice.

And then the light went out of its eyes.

'Is it dead?' Grace whispered, though she already knew the answer. She could feel it. The connection had gone. She felt strangely empty as she looked out at the Leviathan's corpse floating, in an unbroken loop, suspended in its sonic cage.

The Doctor turned to Ketor. 'Congratulations,' he said coldly. 'The Leviathan contained the soundwaves, or slowed their release at least. It saved the marine life for miles around that you would've killed.'

'It would have consumed everything in the ocean if left unchecked,' Ketor retorted. 'I've done my job.'

Suddenly, Grace felt a spark behind her eyes. Like a tiny electric shock, not painful, but alerting her attention to something.

She stared into the Leviathan's dead eyes.

'Doctor,' said Grace, clutching her head. 'I can still feel it. How can I feel it if the Leviathan is…' Her eyes widened as he scanned them with his sonic. 'Doctor, look! It's moving!'

'What?' said the Doctor, spinning round on his heels.

Ketor looked aghast. 'It can't be.'

'It is,' said the Doctor in astonishment.

At first there was only a slight twitch of movement in the Leviathan's tail.

Then its jaw twitched too.

And then its jaw began to open, dislocating as it stretched wide. Something slithered its way out through the mouth of the serpent's corpse. A second, apparently identical creature.

'What the *hell*?' said Ketor.

'How is it doing this?' said Grace.

Tail first, the newly emerging creature began to consume the coiled body of its dead self, slithering round in a loop, sloughing, until there was nothing left of the old, and its entire being had been replaced.

The Leviathan was reborn.

'It's an ouroboros!' breathed the Doctor.

'What's an ouroboros?' Ketor asked.

'The serpent that eats its own tail,' said Grace.

'Ancient and eternal,' said the Doctor. 'It creates and then it destroys. It lives and then it dies. And then it's reborn – regenerated – as itself. Existing for all time in endlessly repeating cycles.'

'You mean...' Ketor hugged himself. 'We can never kill it?'

'Looks that way.'

Outside in the water, the new-born Leviathan was swimming in small concentric circles, already growing in strength, getting used to its new body. Grace stared at it; it stared back. A recognition. Should she be afraid? Would this creature torment her thoughts like before? Would it be worse this time?

'Blasted creature!' exclaimed Ketor.

'Enough with the blasting, please, Ketor,' said the Doctor. 'We don't need to kill it to stop it. Every creature has a weakness. An Achilles' heel. Grace, you've got closer to the Leviathan than anyone. You've reached inside it, somehow, like it reached inside you. Why?'

'Yes,' said Ketor, starting to think. 'Yes, why would it imprint itself on your mind? What's the connection?'

'It's like the sea…' Grace thought aloud.

'Go on…' said the Doctor.

'The sea is wild, chaotic,' she went on. 'Vengeful, destructive, beautiful, all these things. The sea falls calm just as surely as it rises to a storm. We cannot control its moods. We can only try to predict them. React to them.'

'Roll with them like the waves.' The Doctor was pacing in a tight circle. 'The Leviathan is more than a beast. It's a force of nature, like the sea. And who understands the sea better than most?'

'Those who work it,' Ketor suggested.

'And those who live beside it,' said the Doctor. 'Who watch it, always. *Endure* it, always…'

'And accept it,' whispered Grace. 'On its own terms.'

The Doctor was watching Grace closely. 'Like any creature, the Leviathan acts on its instincts, shaped by its environment. By its solitary existence. Maybe sometimes it looks out at those around it. *Reaches* out...'

Grace snorted softly. 'To a lighthouse keeper's daughter on a tiny rock?'

The Doctor smiled. 'Anyone who thinks they're too small to make a difference hasn't spent a night with a mosquito.' He took her gently by the shoulders. 'The Leviathan reached out to someone shaped by her environment, by her solitary existence, who acts on her instincts.'

Ketor frowned. 'It saw itself in *her*.'

'It helped that she was young and strong with a mind wide open,' said the Doctor. 'The *Forfarshire*'s captain saw and... well, he was too terrified to even open his eyes. His mind burnt up.'

'But what was it reaching out for?' Grace asked.

'What any of us is reaching out for,' said the Doctor. 'Connection. It wanted to be seen.'

'All right, so for whatever reason, Grace has formed a bond with the Leviathan,' said Ketor. 'And if that thing trusts her in some way, she can trick it.'

'I... I don't know if I could,' Grace said cautiously.

'You could,' Ketor insisted. 'Lead it into a trap. Something bigger this time, stronger. Something—'

'That will only start the whole life-and-death cycle all over again,' the Doctor interrupted.

'I brought the Leviathan to calm for a time, did I not?' said Grace. 'It is a living creature, when all's said. And even the wildest of creatures may be trained.'

'Trained to act differently!' exclaimed the Doctor. 'Not domesticated, not tamed like a dancing bear. But all creatures evolve. Find a new way of being. So let's see if we can give it a bit of a nudge in the right direction along the way.'

'Talk,' said Ketor dismissively. 'The Leviathan must have looked into the eyes of a million victims before. And no offence to you, Grace, but if all it took to win its sensitive little soul was a lighthouse keeper's daughter on a tiny rock…'

'Perhaps the lighthouse itself plays a part,' said Grace. 'I cannot speak for that poor host of the beast's victims, but both the captain and I were near the lighthouse when we saw it…'

'Did I mention mosquitos?' The Doctor was holding stock still, eyes wide. 'Like a lot of insects, they're drawn to light. Positively phototactic.'

Ketor shrugged. 'So?'

'There's a whole spectrum of light but only a fraction of it is visible to the human eye. Ultraviolet light—' he broke off and turned to Grace – 'sorry, what you'd know as chemical rays…'

Grace remembered her father explaining the concept most enthusiastically some years back. 'Rays of light beyond violet that Herr Ritter discovered?'

'Right. Well, those rays have a shorter wavelength, so humans can't see them. But other creatures can. Like mosquitos.' The Doctor smiled. 'Like...'

'Serpents?' Grace felt her smile start to rival his own. 'So it was the beacon on the lighthouse – the light rays that we can't see – that attracted the Leviathan in the first place?'

'You were just a bonus!' The Doctor laughed. 'Deep sea creatures are susceptible to UV light. It regulates their circadian rhythm, controls their sleep cycles, energy levels, hormones, body temperature, the lot. And that Leviathan out there has just been reborn. What if we could channel UV waves into the Leviathan's brain to regulate its rhythm, influence its nature...'

Ketor looked unimpressed. 'By asking it nicely not to devour all life?'

'Bit more sophisticated than that,' said the Doctor. 'And a bit tricksy to pull off. Tricksy and risky.'

'But if there's a chance to imprint a new mode of behaviour onto that creature,' Grace said, 'I suppose we must take it. Mustn't we?'

'We'd need to shine a UV light into its retina,' the Doctor continued. 'I've got UV lights somewhere in my TARDIS. It won't be strong enough on its own, but we can amplify it with your lighthouse, Grace. We can magnify the UV from the lantern room and use the beam to shine it directly into Levi's eyes.'

'They'd need to be above water,' Ketor pointed out.

'Yes, right. This is where Grace comes in,' said the Doctor. 'We know she can hold its gaze.'

'For a moment!' Grace argued. 'And the pain of it…'

'But that moment became so much more,' the Doctor reminded her. 'You reached out to it before. Calmed it down. If you can do that again while we expose it to the UV, well…' He glanced at Ketor. 'The Leviathan might just see the light.'

Chapter Fifteen
Ultraviolet

Grace paced up and down in the TARDIS, mentally preparing for what she was about to do. 'What about Mam and Father?' she asked suddenly. 'They're still inside the lighthouse. They won't comprehend any of this. And certainly, won't stand back idly and let you meddle with the function of the lamp. If only there were a way they could sleep through the whole thing without a care...'

'Well, since you ask, there is.' The Doctor produced a phial of amber liquid. 'Snooze syrup. It'll give them the best night's sleep they've ever had. They'll wake in the morning refreshed.'

'Well, that is a boon I'll be glad to bestow upon them.' She smiled bravely. 'One way or another, when they wake, our work will be done.'

'And done well!' said the Doctor, spinning the controls.

The TARDIS landed and Grace pushed open the door.

'I'll just be in here,' said the Doctor, rummaging around under the TARDIS's flooring, 'finding the equipment I need for the new beam. Ketor, pass me that box of lightbulbs?'

Grace stepped outside onto Longstone Rock.

It was the island she had lived on her whole life, but today, nothing felt familiar.

She felt alienated. Night was falling, and there was a chilling wind in the air. She hurried up the big stone steps to the lighthouse and heaved open the door.

She had barely set foot inside when her mother smothered her.

'There you are,' Mrs Darling reproached. 'We have been beside ourselves with worry, Grace.'

Mr Darling appeared and stood silently at his wife's side.

'I'm sorry,' said Grace, bowing her head. She knew her parents still clung on to her as much as she clung on to them. And if anything were to happen to her… She couldn't bear to think what that would do to them.

'Disappearing all day without so much as one word,' said Mrs Darling. 'And the coble was gone. We feared you must have drowned. This is most unlike you, Grace. Where on earth have you been?'

'I went to visit Thomasin, in Bamburgh,' Grace lied.

'Oh,' said Mrs Darling, sounding relieved. 'You were with your sister?'

Grace nodded, blushing with guilt. Perhaps, in time, she would be able to tell Thomasin everything for real. Right now, though, she had to protect her family from much more than just the truth.

'What can I do to help calm your nerves, Mam? Milk?' She was already heating some up on the wood stove.

Fear Death by Water

'Thank you, my angel,' Mrs Darling replied, sinking into her rocking chair.

'Father?'

He shook his head. 'I should be attending to the light.'

'No, stay here,' said Grace. 'Sit with Mam for a bit. I'll make you a drink too and attend to the light myself. I've been gone all day. It's the least I can do.'

'Oh Grace, what would we do without you?' Mrs Darling muttered. 'Sit down, William. You've not stopped since dawn.'

Mr Darling relented, taking the chair next to his wife. 'Grace, while you're up there, have a look for the barometer, will you? I can't seem to find it anywhere. I must be going mad.'

'I'll find it, Father.' Grace smiled. 'Now, the two of you simply must try this special tonic I picked up on the mainland.' She ostentatiously slipped a few drops of the Doctor's sleeping syrup into their hot milk. 'I promise you, it's extremely relaxing.'

Mr Darling took the proffered mug and sniffed warily. 'Doesn't smell of much...' He took a good mouthful. 'Doesn't taste of much, either.'

'Let me try some,' said Mrs Darling. She took an enthusiastic sip from her own mug, and smacked her lips. 'Oh, that's lovely...'

In moments the two of them had fallen fast asleep.

Grace gently removed the mugs from her parents' hands, looked at their peaceful faces and smiled.

'I love you,' she whispered, almost weeping.

Then she hurried outside and back into the TARDIS.

The Doctor wound his new hand-knitted scarf around Grace's neck to give her an extra layer. 'Suits you,' he smiled. 'Ready?'

Grace nodded. They all stepped outside onto Big Harcar.

'The coble,' said Grace, seeing that her boat was still on the rock. 'We must return it to the boatshed.'

'Don't worry about that,' said the Doctor. 'I'll take it back in my TARDIS.' He scouted the rock's surface for its highest, centremost point. 'This is your spot, Grace. You'll need to be facing away from the lighthouse so the Leviathan is facing the beam. Ketor, you are in charge of Chip's remote control for the sonic cage.' He handed it over then waggled a curious black metal device the size of a house brick. 'And you'll need this.'

'What is it?' asked Ketor.

'Walkie-talkie,' said the Doctor, 'so we can communicate. Look after it please, Ketor. These two radios are UNIT property.'

Grace shook her head. 'Whatever do you speak of, Doctor?' He opened his mouth to reply and she placed a finger to his lips. 'I know. A million questions, when we are in need of a single answer.'

'Right,' said the Doctor with a grin. 'I need to get to the lantern room, so I can start setting up the UV beam.'

'Doctor...' said Grace sheepishly, following him back to the TARDIS. 'I don't think I can do this.'

'Actually, you are the only person in the world who *can*,' said the Doctor, trying to big her up. 'You're a hero, Grace Darling.'

'I'm not, though,' said Grace, shaking her head. 'I'm a lighthouse keeper's daughter, I'm not a heroine.'

'Why can't you be both? That's one of the most amazing things about you humans: you have the capacity to be two contradictory things at once. A unity of opposites, just like the Leviathan. Chaotic and calm. Fearsome and beautiful. Destructive and creative.'

'Life and death,' said Grace, remembering her earlier conversation with the Doctor in the lighthouse. 'You can't have one without the other.'

'An interconnectedness of all things!' said the Doctor. 'You and the Leviathan are not so different.'

'Is the Leviathan scared? No, it is not,' Grace whispered. 'As for me... I'm terrified.'

'And still doing this anyway. Making you the bravest of the brave.' He put his hand on her shoulder. 'You can do this, Grace. Ketor will help you.' He waved the walkie-talkie. 'And I'm not far away.'

Grace nodded, then the Doctor slipped back inside, shutting the door behind him this time.

Inside the TARDIS, the Doctor leaned against the doors, taking a second to breathe, to think.

Grace is going to be okay, isn't she?
Is this risking future history?

He stripped out of his diving suit and shrugged on his long, leather coat. Then he reset the coordinates for Longstone Rock and pulled the lever.

The TARDIS wheezed and groaned as it dematerialised from Big Harcar Rock and tried and failed to materialise inside the lantern room.

'Come on, old girl,' said the Doctor. The TARDIS was too big to fit inside the glass-enclosed room, alongside the massive beacon.

He was going to have to improvise.

The Doctor hovered the TARDIS in stasis outside the window. He leant out of the window and sonicked opened one of the sections of window. He looked at the gap – at the 80-foot drop below. Then jumped across and tumbled into the lantern room.

He immediately set to work, calculating the mechanics of the beacon. It was going to require some speedy engineering. The Doctor analysed the Argand oil lamps; somehow he needed to convert them into a source that would emit a broader spectrum of light, including UV. He scanned the room. The barometer, he remembered. It was still in his TARDIS and it had given him an idea...

He hopped back out of the window and into his ship.

Back in the console room, he rummaged through the box of lightbulbs for twelve bulbs, borosilicate or something transparent to UV, to allow the specific wavelengths to be transmitted; one to replace each Argand oil lamp.

He could only find seven; that would have to do. Then his gaze landed on his old sonic specs. He grabbed those from the side too, to protect his eyes from the close-range intensity of the UV light.

He jumped back into the lantern room, arms bundled full of borosilicate glass bulbs. With expert precision, the Doctor filled the bulbs' inner tube with small amounts of mercury from the barometer. There was just enough left, after refilling the fluid link earlier. Now he had seven mercury vapour lamps; high-intensity outputs, suitable for large scale applications... like streetlights.

Like lighthouses!

The Doctor wound down the Argand oil lamps, extinguishing their glow, and for a moment the lantern room fell into complete darkness.

'Can't have a lighthouse without light...' said the Doctor, reaching for his sonic. He aimed it at the TARDIS's rooftop lamp and the lantern boosted into a brilliant bright white light. The lantern began to sweep in a circle, shining out for miles around.

Job done, the Doctor crossed to the telescope, aimed and squinted through.

There was Grace standing in the middle of the rock.

Preparing to face her fear.

Chapter Sixteen
The Lady of the Rock

Waves crashed into Big Harcar Rock, splashing Grace with sea spray. Wind swept through her hair, and she was grateful for the extra layer of warmth the Doctor's scarf was providing. She wrapped her shawl tightly around herself. She still felt numb with fear over what she was about to attempt.

All around her, the wind moaned. Or was it the sound of the Leviathan groaning in its sonic cage under the sea? It was hard to tell. Either way, it was eerie. There was a reason she never came over to the rocks at night. They were even more dangerous than usual.

It was dark now. And here she was. Isolated. Alone. Exposed to the elements.

'Are you ready?' asked Ketor, coming over to her side. Grace knew he was here to help her, but his presence made her feel even more alienated.

'I think so.' Grace looked over her shoulder at the lighthouse. The light had gone out, meaning the Doctor must be at work setting up the new beam. The lamp on top of his strange craft was a strong substitute beacon, she thought.

'I'll be just over there,' said Ketor, pointing to the edge of the rock. 'I'll raise the sonic cage so the Leviathan's head can rise above the water. No more than that. The Doctor will activate the beam. The rest is down to you, Grace.'

Grace nodded. 'I understand.'

'Good luck.'

Ketor headed back to the edge, leaving Grace alone. She closed her eyes for a moment to compose herself.

When she opened her eyes, she could see the sea in front of her begin to bubble and boil.

In the lantern room, the Doctor frantically unscrewed the glass Argand oil lamps, replacing seven of them with the borosilicate bulbs. He sonicked the bulbs, and the mercury began heating. The Doctor put on his sonic sunglasses. As the current flowed through the lamp, the vapour produced a spectrum of UV light: UVA, UVB, UVC, even a little visible light.

He adjusted the prisms and rotating mirrors to create a ripple effect with the light, to enhance its rhythmic, hypnotic effect. The light flickered, casting intermittent beams across the dark seascape.

It was too weak. It was taking too long to warm up, to reach its full brightness.

'Come on,' the Doctor muttered. 'Come on, come on, come *on*.' He returned to the telescope to check on the state of play down on the rock.

Fear Death by Water

The waters were bubbling, spray spitting high up into the air. The beast was rising from the deep.

You have to look at it, Grace told herself. She forced herself to open her eyes again.

As she did, the Leviathan reared its colossal head above the waves.

Grace screamed and stumbled a few steps backwards. All she could think of was the ungodly fear she had felt the first time she saw those eyes. And all the dead she had seen in the water in the moments that had followed. *Where were they now? What had happened to their souls?*

The fire-eyes flared in her mind.

Grace wondered: How many times had the Leviathan died and then lived again? Could it ever die?

Does any living creature deserve to die? she thought. *Is there life after death for everyone?*

She raised her head and took in the brutish magnificence of the creature as it surged forwards, then turned back, then coiled sideways, trying to break free of its containment.

Grace bunched her fists and fixed her gaze on the Leviathan, waiting for it to look back at her as it had done twice before. Why wasn't it responding? Perhaps the light from the new beam wasn't strong enough yet.

Hurry up, Doctor!

Or perhaps it was her fault. Maybe the Leviathan wasn't still enough; she wasn't doing a good enough job at keeping it calm. *Is any cage strong enough to hold this force of nature?* she wondered.

Suddenly, Grace sensed an overwhelming frustration to be free. A sense of being suffocated, by the press and public attention that were beginning to invade her life, even inside the sanctuary of her own home. She'd been suppressing it, but now it bubbled up to the fore. The headlines proclaimed her a heroine. She didn't want to be Grace Darling, the heroine, or even Grace Darling the lighthouse keeper's daughter. She just wanted to *be*. Herself. Grace. A simple soul, connected to the sea. The wild and beautiful sea that made her feel so free, connected to creation.

Was that why she had an affinity with the Leviathan, despite the danger that came with it? Here she stood on the wave-bitten rock, surrounded by the vast open ocean but unable to launch out and experience it. For a beast that belonged fully to the sea, the Leviathan must be feeling the same but infinitely stronger. This iteration had been reborn inside this cage, after all. Containment was all it had known, but its every instinct must be screaming to be free.

From the edge of the rock, Ketor could hear Grace shouting. He couldn't quite make it. *Something about the sonic cage…*

'WHAT?' he yelled back.

'I SAID TURN OFF THE CAGE!'

Fear Death by Water

'WHAT? WE CAN'T.'

'YOU WANT THE BEAST TO BE CALM?'

'YES, BUT...'

The Doctor crackled through on the walkie-talkie.

'Ketor, what's happening down there? Talk to me!'

'She's telling me to turn off the cage. But just look at that thing!'

The Leviathan was thrashing in the surf, its teeth biting at the air, its sinuous bulk churning the waters.

'TURN IT OFF!' Grace shouted. 'PLEASE, YOU MUST!'

'Do it, Ketor,' the Doctor said simply. 'Grace knows this creature better than we do.'

'It'll kill all of us!'

'Do it. Keep me on the line.'

Ketor hesitated.

He could drop the radio, hurl it into the sea. Disregard the Doctor and this girl and their idiotic plan.

And yet, if Chip were here, Ketor knew just what he would be saying. Just what he'd said when Ketor had chosen to go his own way and fire up the sonar dome that first time.

'You're not right just cos you say you are! You don't know better than everyone else!'

Grace thought she was right now. Was she making the same mistake?

I wish you were here, little brother, thought Ketor. *You were always the clever one.*

He switched the settings on the remote control. As the sonic cage dissipated, he held his breath.

An almighty, ear-splitting roar echoed around the Farne Islands. Guttural and elemental.

Freed from its cage, the Leviathan coiled and uncoiled, then raised itself from the water like a giant cobra ready to strike, towering over the lighthouse.

Grace trembled. Like David facing Goliath, she had never felt smaller or more afraid.

The Leviathan roared again. Foul grey mucus spat out of its mouth, landing on the surface of the rock with an acidic fizz.

'Grace!' shouted Ketor, running towards her.

Grace held up her hand, never taking her eyes from the Leviathan.

'Stay back!' she thundered.

The Leviathan's eyes ignited, bursting into a blinding molten glow. Fiery orbs, of searing energy. Burning with intense power.

With explosive force, two fireballs shot through its vertical slit pupils, up into the sky.

It was so hot, Grace thought her own eyes might melt. She felt like she was burning up; she could feel the creature's hold over her growing.

Two more fireballs burst forth. Then two more. And more. Fireball after fireball after fireball, projecting into the sky, crashing into the surrounding sea; each impact throwing up plumes of steam and droplets that sizzled in the cold night air.

The Doctor needed to boost the light, and fast. Connect the TARDIS to the beacon, use that as a power source. Quickly, he climbed back out of the window, balancing on the metal railing that ran around the outside of the top of the lighthouse, preparing to jump back across into the TARDIS.

The air crackled with energy, thick with smoke and the sour-musk scent of the Leviathan as sparks rained down around the lighthouse, like a firework display of fiery meteors. The Doctor ducked as a fireball hurtled past him, narrowly missing the lantern room.

The railing wobbled underfoot. The Doctor paused for a moment, bracing against the shockwaves of the celestial bombardment, his hearts racing. The wind tugged at his clothing. Then his left boot slipped off the metal ledge. His right boot too. But his reactions were lightning fast. Catching hold of the railing with both hands, he hung off the metal bar.

Another fireball shot past, so close to his face that he could feel the blistering heat of its blazing trail against his skin. He could feel beads of sweat dripping down his forehead, his entire body prickling with adrenalin. On the rock, he could see the Leviathan looming over Grace.

Suddenly, amidst the crackling of flames, he could hear the hum of drones. There was a clash of fire and metal: advanced alien technology versus the raw fury of nature. Illuminated by the glow of the fireballs, the drones' sleek circular frames moved with precision, their sensors locking onto the blazing orbs. One of the drones fired beams of plasma to disintegrate the flames. The other deployed anti-mavity nets, trapping the fiery balls in translucent webs before flinging them out of the way, back into the upper atmosphere, keeping Grace, the rock and the lighthouse safe.

The Doctor swung his legs from side to side to generate the momentum he needed to claw himself up back onto the ledge. Finally he jumped back into the TARDIS. As he landed, Ketor's voice crackled through the walkie-talkie. 'Doctor...'

He fumbled for the device to reply: 'Excellent work with the drones down there, Ketor! Chip would be proud.'

'I wanted him with me. I guess in a way he is,' Ketor said. 'But what are we going to do? The Leviathan's free and the beam's not strong enough.'

'I know, I know!' said the Doctor, uncoiling a cable from the console. 'I'm working on it!'

'And what about Grace?' said Ketor. 'That thing's too much for anyone to control.'

'Let me talk to her,' said the Doctor.

The Leviathan loomed towards Grace, baring its teeth and opening its huge gaping jaws. It looked ready to destroy her.

Grace's heart was pounding in her chest and her legs felt like lead weights, bolting her to the rock. The rock where so many ships had foundered and so many souls had drowned. Even if she could move her legs, there was nowhere to run.

Is this it? Am I going to die?

Grace looked into the black hole of the Leviathan's gullet. It was a gateway to nothingness, the point of no return.

And in that moment all her hope for life was lost.

She closed her eyes.

Defenceless.

Defeated.

And then she heard the Doctor's voice, breaking through that walkie-talkie device. Ketor was standing next to her, holding it to her ear.

'Grace,' said the Doctor. 'Breathe. Listen to me. This creature isn't going to kill you. Its elemental turmoil is stirring inside you because you're connected. Use that connection. Use your own nature to calm it.'

'But it's too strong,' said Grace, 'too powerful.'

'So are you.'

'I'm afraid.'

'Remember what I told you. Your fear can be your superpower. You're surging with energy right now! Focus that into the Leviathan. You are in control of your thoughts, they are not in control of you.'

Grace felt herself panicking, her breath quickening.

'Deep breaths,' said the Doctor. 'Focus on the sound of the sea. You've got this.'

The Doctor's voice crackled into silence.

The Doctor extended the cable from the TARDIS console towards the door, then, clutching hold of the end, ran and jumped back across into the lantern room one last time. He connected the cable to the mechanics of the beacon. Power surged from the TARDIS into the lantern room, boosting the beam. With a surge of power it began to radiate hypnotic waves of ultraviolet.

'Let there be light!' said the Doctor, punching the air then grabbing the telescope. 'Come on, Grace, hold it… you *must* hold it!'

Grace was doing as the Doctor had said: focusing her mind on the sound of the sea, for a few moments allowing herself to be soothed by the rhythmic roar of the waves she had heard her whole life.

But then the Leviathan's roars resumed, mingling with the howling wind and crashing waves to create an elemental cacophony.

It was deafeningly loud. Too loud to be calm.

Grace stuck her fingers in her ears.

Everything fell quiet.

All she could hear was the strange empty echo of her heartbeat in her ear. She took deep breaths, using the pulse to regulate her breathing.

As she finally began to calm herself, she noticed that the Leviathan too was beginning to calm a little. And as it calmed, it finally caught Grace's gaze. *Two spirits of the sea, psychically bonded.* The Leviathan wasn't looking away. Grace didn't dare to blink. Not even once. She channelled all her mental energy into a single thought: *If the ocean can calm itself, then so can you.*

It's working! Grace could see that the Leviathan was distracted by the ultraviolet light. It began to slow its frantic writhing, mesmerised, its primal instincts shifting and stirring like deepwater currents.

Tentatively, Grace removed her fingers from her ears. She could no longer hear the howling of the wind or the roar of the waves against Big Harcar Rock. What she could hear was a faint blend of low and high frequency, aquatic but ethereal. A distant aeolian tone, filtering through the Leviathan.

Overcome with awe and wonder, Grace remembered that Chip had said the Leviathan flits between the seas of the cosmos. She understood it now. She could hear it. She could *feel* it. The Leviathan was not just connected to her, and to this ocean, but to every ocean in the galaxy. And these were the sounds of their shores.

The flames in the Leviathan's eyes turned green as the process took effect, channelling new thought waves and a new circadian rhythm into the creature's brain. Its movement continued slowing, trance-like as it absorbed the rays, falling under a deep hypnotic influence.

After the longest minute of Grace's life, the fire in the creature's eyes died down. And then the Leviathan blinked, as though seeing the world for the very first time.

Chapter Seventeen
When Life Gives You Potatoes

It was almost alluring, the new glow in the Leviathan's eyes. Grace tracked the illumination as the serpentine figure weaved in and out of the water, playfully circling Big Harcar Rock.

'It's beautiful,' said Grace, as they sat watching, waiting for the Doctor to come and pick them up. She pulled the Doctor's scarf around her neck.

She was exhausted. But the storm in her mind was calm now. And so was the Leviathan.

If it embodies the chaos of the sea then it embodies its wild beauty too, she thought.

'You *were* right,' said Ketor, who was sitting by her side. 'And I was right to listen to you. You tamed it. Now it can be free.'

Grace smiled gratefully at Ketor. He may have been from another sphere, but some things were universal. They sat together in silence for a while.

Ketor stared blankly out to sea, silently drowning in his grief. Somehow feeling heavy and hollow at the same time.

'I lost my brother too,' Grace said eventually. 'Eight years ago. His name was Job. He died at Christmastime, just before his twentieth birthday.'

Ketor still didn't speak, but he was listening, finding himself unexpectedly comforted by Grace's words.

'I asked Father to cancel Christmas. The thought of Christmas without Job didn't feel right. I remember, Father said: "It's not what Job would have wanted. He would have wanted us to celebrate his life and give thanks." So that's what we did: celebrated in his honour, though it was a sorrowful time. I cried every single day at first.'

Ketor looked at Grace and saw that even now she had tears in her big brown eyes. He wished he could cry but it was something he could never seem to do. However much he wanted to.

'Water is the difference between life and death, don't you think?' Grace continued. 'It sustains life and yet too many die in the wake of water. I have found that grief also comes in waves. It ebbs and it flows. Sometimes the waters of grief are calm and other times they're turbulent. We cannot control it; we must simply learn to navigate it. You navigate well, Ketor. You'll be all right.'

She held out her hand for Ketor to hold.

He took it.

'We are children of the water, you and I,' she said.

Ketor could feel a swell of emotion behind his eyes, and at the back of his throat.

In silence, he let out a single tear as he stared out to the ocean, calmed by the steady pulse of the waves, whispering the great secrets of the sea.

Grace could hear the wheezing of the TARDIS behind them. She turned around. There was the Doctor's magical blue box on the old rugged rock. The door creaked open.

'There you are!' she said as he stepped out. 'Where've you been?'

'Night fishing!' the Doctor grinned, proudly presenting a net containing his catch. 'Plenty of herring. There's life in the ocean yet besides the Leviathan. Speaking of which – that was a-*mazing*, team! *You* are amazing, Grace.'

'Where will the beast go now?' Grace wondered, turning back to watch the Leviathan.

'It seems to like this rock,' noted Ketor.

'Perhaps because Grace does?' The Doctor smiled at her. 'I assume you're still connected?'

Grace nodded. She could feel it.

But it was different now.

Elemental. Beautiful.

It didn't just feel like she was connected to the Leviathan. It felt like she was connected to the ocean.

Every ocean.

'What if it stays here?' suggested the Doctor.

'What if it decides to kill again?' countered Ketor.

'It's an ouroboros,' said the Doctor, 'the definition of recreation and everlasting life. It was savage and primordial, but it's evolving, now there's just that little bit of Grace programmed into its psyche. We know she can influence it. So what if it adopts her impulse to prevent ships from navigating into the rocks?'

'You're saying it could use its hydrokinetic powers to control the currents around these rocks?' said Ketor.

A guardian of the Farne Islands? Grace liked the idea. She watched the Leviathan closely as it continued to weave around the rock, making waves. Perhaps that's what it was already doing.

'Ketor can pop by every so often, keep an eye on things,' said the Doctor.

'The ISC will have to agree.' Ketor shuffled awkwardly on the rock. 'I'll have to explain...'

'They don't need to know about the sonar damage,' said the Doctor. 'You've learnt your lesson. I won't tell, if you don't.'

'I'm sorry, Grace,' said Ketor. 'I damaged your ocean's ecosystem. If there's any way I can ever repay that debt...'

'Smell that spoor?' said the Doctor. They breathed in the sour musk. 'Yeah, I know, it's a bit stinky, but I ran a test... the spoor is the Leviathan secreting incredible proteins into the ocean that will speed up breeding in the local wildlife for a limited time. That must be how it sustains its feeding grounds. Great for the fish, harmless to those who feed on them. The population of the North Sea will be back up to speed before we know it.'

'It must be the Lord's work,' said Grace.

'Certainly not the Time Lord's work, for a change,' said the Doctor, waving his net of fish. 'It's time to eat. I'm starving!'

In the lighthouse's kitchen, Grace rummaged around in the pantry to see what she could rustle up to accompany the Doctor's herring. There wasn't much. But she could always rely on a surplus of potatoes from their vegetable patch on Brownsman Island.

'I shall fry the fish and prepare some boiled potatoes,' Grace announced.

The Doctor halted her. 'Grace, *darlin'* – sorry, I've been waiting ages to say that – can I cook the potatoes?'

'But you are a man,' Grace objected.

'Am I?' said the Doctor. 'I can't keep up.'

'Cooking is women's work,' Grace insisted.

'And according to the standards of your time, saving lives at sea is men's work. You're a brilliant contradiction, Grace! I am too. So. Spuds, gimme. I've worked in restaurants. Beat the Master on Satellite Five's *Masterchef*...'

Grace shook her head and passed the potatoes to the Doctor, who tossed the tatties into the air in quick succession and began to juggle.

'I've got an idea of what will go with our fish tonight...'

'Well,' said Grace, tucking into the crispy coating of the fried potato. It was soft and fluffy and hot inside. 'I have never tasted anything so delicious.'

They sat outside on Longstone Rock, eating their midnight feast under the light of a full moon, the stars, and the beacon that shone brightly again at the top of the lighthouse.

'And these potatoes come from the earth, not the sea?' asked Ketor.

'Yes, we grow them in soil,' Grace explained. 'Then we usually boil them or mash them. But we have never fried them before. We have used up Mam's cooking oil with all the frying.'

'Worth every drop!' exclaimed the Doctor, smacking his lips.

A small flight of petrels and albatross swarmed in the night sky, squawking noisily overhead.

'Did you know that some seabirds can sleep while flying?' said the Doctor.

'I didn't know that,' said Grace. 'I heard that seabirds carry the souls of dead sailors to the afterlife and if you see them, it's considered good luck.'

'Do you really believe that?' asked the Doctor.

Grace shrugged. 'I think it's probably just superstition.'

A gull dropping landed on the Doctor's shoulder. The white, paste-like substance dribbled down his arm, and he grimaced.

'See,' Grace chuckled. 'Good luck.'

Ketor even cracked a smile too. That was until a gull swooped down and pinched one of his potatoes. 'Oi!' he shooed. 'Beat it, bufflehead.'

Everyone laughed. Even Ketor. Then he sighed, overcome again with sadness. 'My brother would have loved this.'

'He's with us in spirit, I am sure of it,' Grace said, raising her eyebrows and nodding towards the seagull, which was still pecking away at the stolen morsel on a nearby rock. Ketor looked at the bird.

'Hello, sailor,' he whispered, allowing himself just for a moment to entertain Grace's theory. The bird looked back with its pearly black eyes and squawked.

Grace speared a chunk of deep-fried potato onto her fork and raised it as a toast: 'To Chip!'

'To Chip!'

'What are you going to do now?' Grace asked Ketor after dinner, as they were clearing up the mess the Doctor had made in the kitchen.

'I'm an officer in the Intergalactic Sea Corps,' said Ketor. 'Whatever comes, I will always have a duty to care for the oceans. And I have to return home eventually. Although, without my brother…'

'No one will ever replace Chip,' said the Doctor. 'Just make sure you're not alone for too long. Find a friend.'

'I'll be fine on my own,' said Ketor.

'You should take some of our potatoes,' said Grace, loading some spuds into a cloth sack. 'We have plenty. They're a very hardy food supply.'

'Thalassians are pescatarian,' said Ketor.

'Chips,' said the Doctor with a sparkle in his eye, 'go very well with fish! I suppose you'll be wanting a lift? Seeing as your ship's still inside Levi and I can't see *that* coming out any time soon.'

'Thank you,' said Ketor.

'Give me five minutes,' said the Doctor.

Chapter Eighteen
Amazing Grace

'Doctor,' said Grace, as they made their way back inside the lighthouse to say goodbye. 'There is something that has been bothering me.'

'Just the one thing?'

Grace glanced over at her parents, who were still sound asleep, snoring gently.

'You knew me. When we first met, you got into the coble and you said you were pleased to be meeting me at last, like you already knew me. What did you mean? How did you know my name?'

'A million questions,' said the Doctor with a smile. He led Grace outside again to where the TARDIS had made landfall. 'Fancy a ride?'

They stepped inside. The sensation gave Grace goosebumps every time.

'What about Ketor? You need to take him home…'

'I said I'd be with him in five minutes,' said the Doctor. 'We've got all the time in the world!'

'No,' said Grace, 'we've got five minutes.'

'And in those five minutes, we can go anywhere you like. I can show you anything in the universe. I can take you there right now and have you safely back home in time for yesterday.'

Grace laughed. 'You do talk some peculiar nonsense, Doctor.'

'My ship doesn't just travel through the waves of space. It travels through the waves of time too.'

'What do you mean, travels through time?'

The TARDIS came to a stop, and the Doctor nodded towards the door. Grace walked over to it, hovering in the doorway, almost bringing herself to nudge the door open, then pulling away.

'What's out there? Where are we?'

'Bamburgh,' said the Doctor. 'Northumberland, 29th of May 2025.'

'The *year* 2025? But that's—'

'All waiting for you out there.' The Doctor grinned. 'You asked me how I knew you. I'm a time-traveller. Through those doors, round the corner and along Radcliffe Road, there's a museum. The RNLI Grace Darling Museum.'

She blinked. 'What on Earth can you mean?'

'I mean, you are an incredibly important person, Grace Darling. You. Your story. What you did on the morning of the 7th of September 1838. People will never forget it. It created a ripple effect. You change things, Grace. Your actions raise awareness of the need for better lifeboats to be stationed along the coast of Great Britain. You never stop saving lives.'

Grace stood, stunned.

'You don't have to take my word for it,' the Doctor continued. 'Do you want to see it? It's just on the other side of those doors.'

Slowly, without so much as taking a peep, Grace pulled the door closed, shutting out the future. Then she turned away.

'Sorry,' the Doctor said softly. 'You don't have to see it. Your museum. I got carried away, I shouldn't have—'

'Please, Doctor,' Grace interrupted. 'I can see the excitement in your eyes. Your thirst for adventure. I can see that you want, perhaps even need, someone to share it with.'

The Doctor shuffled uncomfortably.

'But I have no desire for a life like yours,' Grace continued. 'I can't begin to comprehend it. Even a hectic life on the mainland is too much for me. I know where my place is in the world. It's in that lighthouse, on that rock, and I am more than content.'

'Contentment is rare, you know,' said the Doctor. 'Hold on to that.'

'And that adventurous spirit of yours is a wonderful thing. You must never lose it. Truly, Doctor, you are one of the most remarkable people I have ever met.'

'Likewise,' the Doctor smiled. 'Grace Darling! The Darling of the Nation.'

Grace winced. 'You read the papers.'

'Now and then,' said the Doctor. 'Thank you, Grace.'

'What for?'

'For standing up to the Leviathan. For rescuing the *Forfarshire* survivors from the rock. I couldn't save them. But you could. And you did.'

'Oh,' Grace replied, modestly. 'It's what anyone would have done.'

'It isn't, though. Honestly. I've seen enough of the universe to know. You can keep telling yourself you're not a hero all you like, but what you did was extraordinary and it will never be forgotten. Quite right too.' He stretched his arms out for a hug. 'Can I?'

Beaming, Grace stood up and wrapped her arms around the Doctor.

'Look after yourself,' he said. 'Keep the light burning.'

'I will. Until my dying day. Please don't be a stranger, Doctor. You are welcome at Longstone any time.'

'I'll check in on you sometimes.'

'I shall look forward to it.' Grace unwound the Doctor's scarf from her neck. 'I believe this is yours.'

'Keep it,' said the Doctor. 'I've already got one. Besides, it looks really good on you.' He turned back to the TARDIS controls and reset the coordinates to 1838. The ship's machinery briefly chugged up and down before it fell still again.

'There,' he said. 'Home again.'

Grace smiled gratefully. 'Thank you. Farewell, Doctor.'

'Goodbye, Grace Darling.'

'Fair winds and following seas.'

Chapter Nineteen
Sir Duke

18 November 1838
Alnwick, Northumberland

The cobbled streets of Alnwick bustled with the cheerful hubbub of morning conversation as eager shoppers congregated around market stalls. Grace eyed the cornucopia of produce on sale: fruit and vegetables; butter and cheese from the local dairy farm; freshly milled flour; baked goods; bunches of flowers; reams of beautiful cloth. This marketplace was the beating heart of Northumberland, a world apart from island life. To Grace, the mainland felt like another planet.

She heard an unfamiliar voice calling her name.

'Grace!' they shouted. 'Look, it's Grace Darling! There she is! It's really her!'

All of a sudden, a crowd of townsfolk swarmed around her. Pushing and shoving to catch a glimpse, shouting her name, grabbing her clothes, pulling her hair. Grace felt herself drowning within a sea of bodies. They were crushing her. She could feel herself starting to panic. She shut her eyes. Her heart was racing.

Then a hand grabbed her sweaty palm. Grace gasped.

'Hold on!' the Doctor whispered into her ear.

'You!' She held on to the Doctor, relieved to see a familiar face.

'Out of the way!' the Doctor shouted, as he pulled Grace through the crowd. 'Move please, thank you!'

Mrs Darling emerged through the dispersing crowd, Mr Darling hot on her heels. 'Grace! What's all this commotion? Oh, hello again,' she said, seeing the Doctor. 'This is unexpected.'

'Hello, Mrs D,' the Doctor replied.

'What are you doing here?' asked Mrs Darling.

'Finally,' said the Doctor, 'I'm returning your barometer. Refilled with mercury. Better late than never, hey.'

Grace rolled her eyes.

The Doctor handed the barometer over to Mr Darling, who frowned at the device. 'That's where it went! But what—'

'Come on,' said Grace, 'let's get away from all these people.'

'Yes, yes,' said Mrs Darling, 'hurry! We don't want to be late for the duke.'

'The duke?' asked the Doctor, following the Darlings.

Mrs Darling looked like she was going to burst with pride. 'My William and Grace have been invited to have a special private reception with the Duke of Northumberland. They are to be presented with the Royal Humane Society's gold medallion for bravery.'

'A well-deserved award!' said the Doctor, grinning. 'Congratulations!'

'Thank you,' said Grace, though she could feel her face flushing. She found it all quite overwhelming.

'It takes a very special occasion for us all to be away from the lighthouse at the same time,' said Mrs Darling.

'Oh, who is looking after the lighthouse?' asked the Doctor. 'I can go and keep an eye on things if you like. The TARDIS is just parked round the corner...'

'We've left my youngest brother, William Brooks, in charge,' said Grace. 'I think he rather fancies himself as a keeper one day. I suspect he shall take after Father.'

Together, the four of them walked along Narrowgate towards Alnwick Castle. Grace stalled a short distance from the thick oak gate of the first bailey surrounding the keep, overcome by how awkward she suddenly felt.

What am I – a plain lighthouse keeper's daughter – doing here? She felt like such an imposter.

'Come along, Grace,' said Mrs Darling. She was several steps ahead, overexcited by the occasion.

'Come in with me?' Grace asked the Doctor.

The Doctor grinned. 'With pleasure.'

'Your Grace,' said Grace, curtsying to the duke in the spotless courtyard.

Hugh Percy, the third Duke of Northumberland, was taller than she had imagined, though he wasn't at all imposing.

He had a friendly face, framed by long sideburns. Dressed in a frock coat and trousers, with a top hat, he stood in impeccably shiny black shoes and leant on a stick, though he couldn't have been much older than her father.

'I rather believe that *you're* Grace,' said the duke with a smile. 'No need for any of that curtsying nonsense. What an honour it is to make your acquaintance, at last, Miss Darling. Mr and Mrs Darling.' The duke looked quizzically at the Doctor. 'And who is this?'

'This is the Doctor, Your Grace.'

'Your Grace.' The Doctor bowed his head. 'How about we cut down on the Graces and I call you something else. How about Sir Duke? Sounds good.'

'You may address me as *Lord* Duke. And you are Doctor who?'

'Oh, I like you already, Sir – sorry – *Lord* Duke.'

'The Doctor is also a Lord,' said Grace.

'Of which manor?' asked the duke.

The Doctor flashed a leather wallet at the duke, who viewed the piece of paper inside sceptically. 'You're my new physician?'

'That's right,' replied the Doctor, with a wink at Grace.

'The Doctor helped us with the injured *Forfarshire* survivors,' explained Grace. 'Though he was one of the survivors himself.'

'Shouldn't really have got involved, but… well, you know how it is.'

'I see,' said the duke.

He looked the Doctor up and down, intrigued though clearly not yet convinced by him.

'Doctor, I thank you for your service. Darlings, would you care to come through? The physician can wait out here. I shall send my adviser to interview him shortly.'

'Adviser! I do that too, by the way!'

The duke led Grace and her parents through a labyrinth of castle corridors. Eventually, they entered a palatial Italian Renaissance-style drawing room, ornately furnished with a carved, painted and gilded ceiling, a marble fireplace and an elaborate overmantle mirror.

'I cannot think of anyone more deserving of the Royal Humane Society's golden medallions,' said the duke, placing a medal on Mr Darling's chest and then on Grace's. 'This is an historic first, in fact: never before has an official British gallantry medal been awarded to a female recipient, and a civilian.'

'I am most honoured, Your Grace,' said Grace, glancing down at the shiny medal. She beamed with a mixture of pride and embarrassment.

'I was not the only one who was impressed,' the duke continued. 'Do sit down and I shall explain.'

Grace perched between her parents on a luxuriously padded red and gold bench as a maid laid out a sumptuous selection of tea and cake she had ever laid eyes on.

The duke sat opposite. 'Miss Darling,' he said with a knowing smile, 'news of your heroism reached

Buckingham Palace. It inspired Queen Victoria herself to send you a gift of fifty pounds.'

Grace didn't know what to say. Mrs Darling clapped her hands to her face in astonishment.

'Now. Please,' said the duke, gesturing for his guests to partake of the refreshments. Grace helped herself to an enormous slice of raspberry tart, unsure how she was going to manage it all.

'I'm sure it hasn't escaped your notice that you've made quite an impression on the British public, Grace,' the duke continued, tucking into his fruit-and-nut cake. 'It has also been brought to my attention that your story has now spread across Europe, and even as far as America, Australia and Japan. I can see that you have been catapulted to a great fame which nothing could have possibly prepared you for. This must have come as quite a shock to you.'

'I must admit, it has,' said Grace, picking at her tart.

Mr and Mrs Darling nodded in agreement.

'I would like to ask your parents if they might allow me to become your guardian. Your patron. It would be my honour to aid you with your finances. I would assign trustees and lawyers to look after your affairs. To shield you, where possible, from unsuitable requests. I know the ways of the world: there will be people wishing to exploit you to profit from your fame. I give you my word that I would do everything in my power to support and assist you. What do you say?'

'Thank you, your Grace,' said Mrs Darling, without hesitation.

'We would be most delighted to accept your offer,' said Mr Darling.

Grace's mind whirled as she was escorted out to the castle's courtyard while her parents continued to discuss matters with the duke. She needed air. She scanned the grounds for the Doctor. No sign. Perhaps he was still in the castle, being interviewed for an imaginary appointment. More likely he'd been thrown out with a flea in his ear for his deception. Grace felt bad for him.

There was so much she wanted to talk to him about. Her life had changed a lot since she last saw him, though it was only a couple of months ago. She wondered if her life would ever be the same again.

She waited, enduring furtive glances from the gardener while enjoying the fruits of his labours: the scent of the freshly cut grass and hybrid tea roses were balm to her soul.

She waited, until her parents finally emerged from their meeting with the duke, and it was time for them to leave. But the Doctor never appeared.

Grace sighed. This seemed to be his way: disappearing here and reappearing there.

She wondered if she would ever see him again.

Chapter Twenty
Time and Tide

12 October 1842
Alnwick, Northumberland

Darkness. Infinite, lonely darkness. Suddenly: a pair of eyes flashed open. They gaped. Ogling. Unblinking. Intimidating. Then another pair of eyes. Then another. And another. And another. Another. Another. Hundreds of pairs of eyes piercing through the pitch black of a nightmare.
All staring at Grace Darling.

Grace opened her eyes. She was shaking all over, covered in a cold sweat. She looked around the room suspiciously, paranoid that she was being watched. *There's no one else here*, she reassured herself. *It was just a nightmare. You're safe. You're in Alnwick. You're with your sister, Thomasin.*

Thomasin always made her feel, not better, necessarily, but certainly less alone. Grace had become a recluse in recent months, retreating into herself in an attempt to evade the public's unrelenting curiosity about her. Wherever she went, people stared. They had even begun turning up to Longstone Lighthouse by the boatload in the hope of a tour of the island from 'Grace Darling the heroine' herself. There was a constant pressure to attend events. Her likeness was on all sorts of souvenirs, without her say: on tins of tea, on soap, plates, postcards, figurines. She had become a product. A product of obsession.

A loud knocking on the front door made Grace jump. *Not again.* It was the fourteenth time this day. Grace heard the echo of footsteps and the sound of Thomasin's voice answering the door.

'You can't see her!' said Thomasin.

'We heard the famous Grace Darling has come to Alnwick,' called a voice from the crowd.

How have they found out I'm here?

'I respectfully ask that you stop knocking and leave.'

'But we've come so far to see her.'

'We just want a lock of her hair.'

Grace didn't have much hair left. She had given it all away. And she no longer had the strength to fend off the crowds herself. Thomasin did that for her. *Dear Thomasin.* Grace wondered what she would do without her.

'I'm sorry,' Thomasin replied firmly. 'She is not at all well. She needs to recover her strength in peace.'

'Please!'

'No. Good day.'

The door slammed shut.

Grace had overheard the same conversation from her bedchamber every day since she'd come here to recover. She had caught a chill in the spring, which led to a persistent cough and a terrible fever. Thomasin had insisted she come to stay with her at their cousins' house in Alnwick, where there were fewer stairs than the lighthouse, even if there weren't fewer visitors. The trouble was, Grace wasn't getting better; she was getting worse.

There was yet another knock at the door.

The fifteenth visitor. Thomasin let them in.

'Hello, Grace,' came a familiar voice.

'Doctor,' she gasped. 'What are you doing here?'

'The Duke of Northumberland has sent his most trusted physician to see you,' he replied, smiling as he knelt down next to Grace's bedside.

Grace smiled. 'The dear duke.'

'He told me you've kept in touch,' said the Doctor.

'Indeed. We correspond often. He has been incredibly kind. You know, he set up a trust fund for me? It has collected nearly a thousand pounds. I do not know what to do with such a sum of money.'

'Well, between you and me, Sir Duke has great plans to use his own fortune to develop safer lifeboats. All thanks to you.'

'Perhaps I shall do the same...' Grace mused. Overcome by a coughing fit, she gasped for air. 'Water. I need water.'

The Doctor took the cup from Grace's bedside table and held it for her, carefully tipping the drink so she could take small sips. The cool liquid slipped down her throat, soothing her prickly cough. 'More?'

Grace shook her head. She looked intently at her old friend, absorbing his face, as though she couldn't quite believe she was seeing it. Or perhaps as though she knew she was seeing it for the last time.

'I began to think that I was never going to see you again,' she rasped. 'I have so very often thought of you and your magical blue wardrobe.'

'How is Levi?' asked the Doctor.

'Guarding the Farne Islands magnificently. Not a single ship has crashed onto the rocks since the *Forfarshire*.' Grace paused. 'Mrs Dawson's dear children passed away.'

The Doctor looked crestfallen. 'When?'

'Last year,' Grace replied. 'Matilda passed first, and then James followed. I feel awful for poor Sarah.'

The Doctor sighed. 'Saving lives... and losing them...'

'We must be grateful for the time we have on this Earth,' said Grace. Then she paused, taking in the Doctor. 'You know, I came to convince myself that you and our peculiar adventure had all been but a dream. Yet here you are...'

'Life is a dream. Sometimes we wake up enough to realise that.'

'And death is but the next adventure,' added Grace. 'Perhaps that is when we truly wake up. Doctor... They say I have consumption.'

The Doctor held Grace's hand in his. His palm was warm and comforting against her ice-cold fingers. Grace screwed her eyes shut.

'Are you in pain? Are you still having visions? The Leviathan?'

'No, that evil eye is gone now. These days I have nightmares of being watched... by ordinary people.'

'You know they look at you because they look up to you,' said the Doctor. 'You're an inspiration, Grace. A hero. That's how they see you.'

'I wish they wouldn't,' said Grace, opening her eyes. 'Sorry.' She shook her head. 'I don't mean to be melancholy. I am dying. Perhaps none of it matters any more.'

'Of course it matters. Hey, I want to show you something.' The Doctor retrieved a small handheld screen from his pocket and held it in front of Grace.

It showed bright moving images – in colour! Images of Ketor, standing in a vast aquamarine hall filled with so many people, receiving an award for services to aquakind:

'I dedicate this award firstly to my late and much-missed brother, Chip. I continue my work in his honour, in his name. Secondly, I dedicate this accolade to an old acquaintance: Grace Darling, citizen of Earth. I wouldn't be standing here accepting this award – indeed, I wouldn't be the Sea Marshal I am today – were it not for her extraordinary act of bravery and compassion in the handling of the Leviathan. Back then, at the beginning of my career, I was naive and reckless and I made mistakes. But what I learnt from Grace on that mission changed me, and I carry it with me, in my work and in my life.'

'Oh,' said Grace, overcome. 'What an unexpected honour.'

'Grace Darling,' the Doctor beamed, 'a ripple in the North Sea making waves across the galaxy.'

'Doctor, I feel I am too young to die,' said Grace, her voice cracking.

'Your spirit lives on, Grace, in so many ways,' said the Doctor. 'Your legacy makes a difference. Be proud of that.'

Grace smiled weakly, recomposing herself. 'I used to be afraid of dying. In fact, I have spent the last four years of my life feeling quite inexplicably afraid. Of what, I am not entirely sure. All I know is that my anxieties have crushed me, terribly so.'

'I'm so sorry,' said the Doctor, tears welling in his eyes. 'I'm sorry I couldn't save you from that.'

'Please don't cry, Doctor,' she said. 'Don't feel sad for me. For as I lie here now, this world around me is fading away and all my worries with it. I don't feel so scared any more. You ask me if I'm afraid and at last my answer is no. Rest assured, as I will rest assured, that I am at peace. I have faith and I have hope.

'At the end of my life, at the end of it all… I do not fear death.'

Epilogue

New Year's Day, 2025
Battersea Park, London

It was a chilly January dawn and the smell of petrichor filled the early-morning air.

Emily sat, sipping her coffee, on her favourite bench in Battersea Park. She often came to this spot, to read or to write or to get lost in her thoughts.

The bench was perfectly positioned next to a magnificent Turkey oak tree by the River Thames, about 90 metres from the Peace Pagoda. It was completely tranquil, save for the occasional chirping of small birds.

There was usually no one else around so early in the day.

However, on this particular morning, a young man walked by and stopped at the tree.

Emily acknowledged the stranger with a subtle smile. 'Happy New Year,' she said.

The stranger smiled back. 'Happy New Year. What year is this?'

Emily chuckled. 'Heavy night, was it? It's 2025.'

'2025. Right. Of course it's 2025.'

Emily considered the man and his odd remark as he sat down on the bench next to her, recollecting a distant memory she couldn't quite place.

'Sorry, do I know you?' she asked.

'Me? I'm just an old wayfaring stranger, travelling through.'

'You look familiar, that's all,' said Emily.

'I've just got one of those faces,' said the stranger. He smiled again. The most brilliant, dazzling smile. Emily smiled back then continued to sip her coffee.

A robin landed on the arm of the bench then it hopped over to the foot of the oak tree and started digging around in the damp soil, hoping to catch something for breakfast. Success! The early bird gobbled its worm and sprang triumphantly onto a plaque that stood in front of the tree trunk:

This tree was planted in Nov. 1938 to commemorate the exploit of GRACE DARLING who at 7 A.M. on Sept. 7th, 1838 rowed with her Father WILLIAM DARLING to the wreck of the steamer Forfarshire and rescued 9 survivors.

'Grace Darling,' said the stranger, reading the plaque.

'You heard of her?' Emily asked.

'Oh, I've heard of Grace Darling!' replied the stranger. 'Really, that plaque should say *12* survivors. But the waves of time wash us all clean. If you remember your loofah.'

Emily raised an eyebrow. 'What are you talking about?'

'Nothing!' He smiled suddenly, self-consciously. But his eyes stayed sad.

'My ancestors were lighthouse keepers,' Emily told him. 'It turns out that Grace Darling is a distant relative of mine.'

'Seriously?'

'Genuinely!'

'Wow! There *is* always a twist at the end,' the stranger muttered to himself.

'I'm researching her for a book I'm writing,' Emily continued.

'Oh, I can tell you a story and a half about Grace Darling.'

'You can? I'd love to hear it. I often wonder about Grace's story. How she would have told it in her own words. Whether she would have told it at all if the media hadn't got involved. How times don't change…'

'Times *do* change,' said the stranger. 'But do you know what doesn't?'

Emily shook her head.

'Humanity's yearning for a hero.'

'What do you mean?'

'I mean, you lot, you're obsessed with stories of heroes and heroines.'

'Maybe. Grace never saw herself as a hero, though.'

'I know. Doesn't mean she wasn't one. She was courageous. Selfless. Scared. Kind. She risked her life to save others. Enough said.'

'She was only 26 when she died,' Emily reflected.
'It's what you do with the years you have that counts.'
'I suppose.'
Emily contemplated the old Grace Darling Oak.
'Does it make you think of life or death? This tree?'
'Oh, life,' the stranger replied. 'Very definitely life. *Always* life.'
'Me too,' Emily smiled.
As she gazed thoughtfully at the tree, the stranger on the bench took out a harmonica from his pocket. 'Stevie Wonder gave me this,' he said.
'*The* Stevie Wonder?' said Emily.
'The one and only.' He kissed the harmonica. 'Best instrument in the world. Fits in your pocket. Oozes with soul. Listen.'
The stranger began playing an old familiar tune. 'Amazing Grace'. Emily closed her eyes and listened to the sweet sound as it echoed around the park. Something about that moment – that man, that tree, that tune – stirred her soul.

Through many dangers, toils and snares, we have already come.
'Twas Grace that brought us safe thus far, and Grace will lead us home.

'So,' said Emily, when the man had finished playing. 'Tell me that story.'

Author's Note

On the evening of Thursday 20 October 1842, Grace Horsley Darling died of tuberculosis in her father's arms at her sister's house in Bamburgh.

She was just 26 years old.

Her funeral took place four days later at St Aidan's Church, Bamburgh. It was attended by hundreds of people wishing to pay tribute to Grace. Her remains rest in the church's graveyard, within a hundred metres of the cottage she was born in on 24 November 1815.

Grace's early death sealed her legendary status. Her story raised public awareness of maritime safety. All the money gifted to Grace in the aftermath of the *Forfarshire* rescue was donated to the development of safer lifeboats and improvement of lifeboat services along the British coast.

On 5 October 1854, the Duke of Northumberland rebranded the modern Royal National Lifeboat Institution. As President of the RNLI, he hoped the charity would continue in the spirit of Grace's heroic actions, and save many lives at sea for years to come.

In 1880, Grace's sister Thomasin published *Grace Darling: Her True Story*, a compilation of Grace's letters, which she hoped would correct the many sensationalised accounts of Grace's life and dispel myth-making.

Today, Grace's legacy continues to live on through the RNLI. Lifeboat crews embody the same values Grace exhibited so boldly in 1838. Grace's memory is honoured and preserved, and the RNLI Grace Darling Museum in Bamburgh is dedicated to her story.

Acknowledgements

This novel would not exist without its marvellous editor, Steve Cole. I am hugely grateful to him for his consistently superb notes, and for the joy it was to bounce ideas around together. Thanks, too, to *Doctor Who*'s brand manager James Page for his infectious enthusiasm, and to Katie Fisher at BBC Books, for being so lovely and ensuring the smooth running of this project.

Special mention must go to Andrew Lewis, Heritage Development Manager at the RNLI Grace Darling Museum in Bamburgh, for granting me access to the museum's private collection of rare books about Grace. Also to Alison, one of the museum's volunteers, who very kindly arranged for me to visit Horsley Cottage, where Grace was born. Thank you Maggie, for welcoming me into your home and helping me feel close to Grace.

I have endless love and appreciation for my dearest friends who support me through everything I do, especially: my brilliant housemate, George Naylor; Nicole McKeever; Jacob Dudman; Emma Bates; Rachel Wicks; Scott Handcock; Rebecca, Charlotte and Rosanna Hiller; Gavin and Kirsteen McGee and Miriam Margolyes.

I am so lucky to have you all in my life.

In addition, I will always be grateful to Peter Ware, Tom Spilsbury, Lizo Mzimba and everyone at *Doctor Who Magazine* for their ongoing encouragement (both professionally and personally) and friendship since the day I started at Panini, fresh out of university. I have been able to write this book because you guys believed in me at the beginning.

Thank you to Peter Harness, my wonderful boss, who inspires me every day with his tremendously intelligent and creative mind. I also want to acknowledge Russell T Davies and Steven Moffat, for capturing my young imagination with their extraordinary *Doctor Who* stories, and for the invaluable advice they have given me in recent years. I take none of it for granted.

Lastly, but most importantly, my family. My sisters, Abi and Josie; you're both amazing and you make me burst with pride. And, of course, my Mum and Dad – Sam and Geoff – who have unconditionally loved and nurtured me, my ideas and my love of language since I was small. Thank you for everything. I adore you more than I can ever say.

This story is for you and for our ancestors.

Also available from BBC Books

DOCTOR WHO

SPECTRAL SCREAM

HANNAH FERGESEN

DOCTOR WHO

RUBY RED

GEORGIA COOK

DOCTOR WHO

CAGED

UNA McCORMACK

BBC

DOCTOR WHO

THE CHURCH ON RUBY ROAD

ESMIE JIKIEMI-PEARSON

TARGET

DOCTOR WHO

73 YARDS

SCOTT HANDCOCK

BBC

DOCTOR WHO

ROGUE

KATE HERRON & BRIONY REDMAN